# GRACE
## unplugged

# GRACE
## unplugged

a novel by
Melody Carlson

**B&H**
PUBLISHING GROUP
Nashville, Tennessee

978-1-4336-8204-9

Published by B&H Publishing Group
Nashville, Tennessee

Dewey Decimal Classification: F
Subject Heading: SINGERS—FICTION \ CHRISTIAN
ETHICS—FICTION \ POPULAR MUSIC—FICTION

1 2 3 4 5 6 7 8 • 17 16 15 14 13

# Chapter 1

With guitar case in hand and only one thing on her mind, Grace Trey shoved open the door that led to the church parking lot and, in her hurry, nearly barreled over the boy just coming in.

"Hey, Noah." Grace steadied the nine-year-old to his feet. "Sorry, bud, I didn't even see you there. What's up?"

"Hey, Miss Grace," he said shyly.

Her frown was replaced with a smile. "Where's my hug?" she asked as she rested her guitar case against her leg and opened up her arms.

Noah responded with a bear hug that melted away the last fragments of her foul mood. "You practicing?" she asked with the directness of a dedicated instructor.

"Yeah." He nodded eagerly. "Every day."

"Good, the recital's coming fast."

"You gonna be there?" he asked with hopeful eyes.

"Of course. You're my star student." She patted him on the shoulder.

Noah grinned and promised to keep practicing. And Grace picked up her guitar, watching as he dashed off to join his friends. She knew the kids were headed for the playground behind the church. There they would roughhouse and compete and joke around until their parents yelled that it was time to go home.

She remembered when she used to do the same thing with her church friends. And sometimes, especially on days like today, she wished she could turn back the clock and run and play with the kids. Life had been so much simpler back then. Okay, maybe it hadn't always been simple, but it was a lot less complicated than trying to be an adult. Although *some* people didn't think of her as an adult.

Despite the fact she was eighteen and, according to the law, old enough to vote or enlist in the armed forces, in her conservative family Grace was still considered a child. Or so it seemed at times. Like today. As she walked through the parking lot, she told herself not to obsess over how Dad had treated her during worship this morning. And yet it was like she couldn't stop.

Worship had started out typically, with their usual six-piece band playing. Grace knew as well as anyone how the congregation loved it when her dad led on guitar. After all, he was Johnny Trey—the guy who'd had a hit record back in his day. But, unless it was her imagination, the congregation seemed to light up even more when the father and daughter duo led worship together. It was like the energy in the sanctuary changed—almost like the congregation expected something special. And naturally Grace wanted to give it to them. However, Dad saw things differently.

Sometimes it felt like she could never do anything right *in his eyes.* Like today. It had felt so right to speed up the tempo and increase the volume on that particular song—she couldn't help herself. And she wasn't blind—she noticed how the crowd reacted. Many of them seemed to appreciate her style. Especially the younger ones. They liked rocking out and worshipping with enthusiasm. What was wrong with that? But just as she was really getting into it, Dad had shot her the look—the look that said, *Knock it off.*

Grace sighed as she glanced around the crowded parking lot, trying to remember where Dad had parked their SUV this morning. She shaded her eyes, peering into the sunshine and wishing she'd driven herself today. That way she could've made a quiet escape without risking more lectures on the way home.

"Hey, superstar."

Grace turned to see her friend Rachel on her heels. "Hey, Rach." She stopped, waiting for her to catch up.

"You really rocked today," Rachel said as she joined her.

"Glad *you* thought so."

"Actually, what I meant was . . ." Rachel's mouth twisted to one side as if she was weighing her words. "I mean, well, it was pretty lively in there for awhile."

"And lively is good, right?" Grace frowned at her best friend.

Rachel shrugged. "Sometimes. Not always."

"Isn't lively better than falling asleep during worship?" Grace frowned.

"I don't know. I think rocking out might make some of the older folks uncomfortable."

"Speaking of older folks." Grace tipped her head to where her parents were strolling their way.

Rachel laughed. "Your parents aren't old folks."

"Guess that depends on your perspective." Now Grace heard the door clicking unlocked, so she opened up the back of the SUV and slid in her guitar case.

"I better get going," Rachel told her.

"I'll come by the bookstore tomorrow," Grace said. "You working?"

"Always." Rachel waved. "See ya."

Grace slipped into the backseat and, slumping down, she went into invisible mode as she stared at her iPhone. Her seemingly oblivious parents chatted congenially as they got in. They made the usual small talk about church and friends they'd visited with, and after a bit they started discussing today's sermon. Occasional comments were tossed her direction, but her one-word answers didn't exactly encourage conversation. She stared out the window, surveying the sleepy streets of Homewood, Alabama. This place wasn't exactly bustling during the week, but on Sunday it felt like a ghost town.

"You're being awfully quiet," Mom said to her. "Everything okay?"

"Everything's fine." Of course, whenever Grace used the *fine* word, it had a completely different meaning.

"You know, Grace, the day will come when you'll miss us," her dad said in a teasing tone. "Next year when you're off at college, you'll think back to these times and—"

"I don't plan to go to college," she said abruptly. Okay, she hadn't meant to break it to them like this, but maybe it was time.

"*What?*" Mom turned to look at her.

"I don't plan to go to college," she repeated the dreaded words.

"Of course, you plan to go to college. You've already been accepted at—"

"I'm not going," she declared.

"Why not?" Mom asked.

"Because I want to do music—"

"Here we go again," Dad said flippantly.

"Don't make fun of me," she told him. "I'm eighteen, and I'm old enough to make up my own mind about my own life. I *want* a music career. Going to college is not going to—"

"A music career is fine—*after* college," he said firmly.

"You know how hard it is for musicians," Mom tried. "You need something to fall back on, Gracie. Like teaching music. You are a fabulous teach—"

"Yeah, right. Or haven't you heard—the ones who *teach* music are the ones who can't *do* music?" Grace snapped.

"Don't disrespect your mother," Dad warned.

Fortunately, he was just pulling up into the driveway, and this doomed conversation was about to end.

"Sorry, Mom," she said quickly. Then, as the garage door slowly opened, Grace jumped out of the SUV. Hurrying around back, where she knew the patio door was unlocked, she let herself into the house and dashed up to her room. Yes, she knew it was childish to play the I-wanna-be-alone game. But besides needing some space, she hoped to get her parents' attention. She wanted them to see that she was serious. She did not want to go to college, and they could not force her. Could they?

Wasn't eighteen old enough to do as you pleased? And what about all the other singers who'd launched fabulous careers while still in their teens? Why wouldn't her parents want that for her? Why would they insist on holding her back? She closed the door to her room, kicked off her shoes, and turned on her laptop. If she couldn't own her music career now, when could she? And putting off her career until she finished four years of useless college made absolutely no sense. She knew college grads who were working at Starbucks and McDonald's. Is that the dream her parents had for her?

She took her laptop to the chair by her window. It was still on the same celebrity gossip blog she'd been reading last night. Sally Benson was a popular blogger on WideSpin.com, and as usual, Sally was up on the latest scoops in the music industry. Grace went back to reading about her favorite performer, Renae Taylor. Renae was in her late twenties and had been enjoying a music career of nearly a decade. Right now, according to Sally Benson, Renae was vacationing in Tahiti, where she was writing songs for her next album. And some paparazzi had managed to snag some pretty cool shots of this megastar on the beach as well as enjoying the nightlife there. *What a life*, Grace thought as she pulled on her headphones, clicking onto one of Renae's most recent songs.

She was just getting into the lyrics when she noticed her door opening. Jerking off her headphones, she glared at the intruder, which she expected was Dad. Didn't he believe in privacy anymore?

"Sorry," Mom said as she stepped inside. "I knocked, but I guess you didn't hear me."

"Oh." Grace nodded.

"Here's your guitar." Mom leaned it against her desk and then lingered there.

"Thanks." Grace started to put her headphones back on.

"Just a minute." Mom held up her hand.

"What?"

"About college," Mom frowned. "I understand how you feel, Grace, but surely you can see our side too. We know the importance of education. I think you do too. You've worked hard in high school. You're a good student. The next natural step for you is college. Surely you can see that."

Grace shrugged. "Not really."

"I think we need to talk about this some more, don't you?"

She bit her lip. Mostly she did not want to have this conversation now.

"We love you, sweetie. We want what's best for you."

"Maybe doing music is best for me."

Now Mom launched into a mini-lecture about how many starving musicians there were in this country. But Grace just tuned her out. She'd heard it all before. Finally Mom must've gotten the message because she glanced at her watch. "Well, Dad and I are heading over to the Fulton's twenty-fifth anniversary at two. It's supposed to be quite a shindig." She made a goofy smile. "You're welcome to join us, if you like."

Grace smirked to think of the slightly stuffy neighbors down the street—she could just imagine how that "shindig" was going down. "Thanks, but no thanks, Mom."

The Fulton's anniversary party must've been an all-day affair because it was after dark when Grace heard her parents come home. She was actually feeling a little left out and had been tempted to go down the street to see what was going on. But now that her parents were home, she was determined to continue her pity party of one. And, really, it was more than that. She was making a stand—a stand for independence. If a girl couldn't make a stand like this at eighteen, when could she? Eventually her parents would have to listen.

Hearing a quiet knock at her door, she turned off the music playing on her laptop and clicking over to e-mail, braced herself, as she told the knocker to "come in." The stand—or perhaps standoff—was about to begin. And she was ready.

"Hey," Dad said gently as he came into her room.

"Hey," she said back, feeling caught off guard by his exceptionally friendly tone. Was it possible he was having a change of heart? But just in case, she kept her eyes on her laptop, pretending to be checking e-mail. She did not want to look directly into his eyes. Sure, at times she hated his conservative parenting ways, but most of the time she loved him, and she knew he could break down her resolve in minutes if he said the right things.

"Listen, about what you said in the car."

"What? You're right; I'm wrong. I get it." She tried to sound nonchalant, but she heard the antagonism in her voice. She wasn't going to let him soften her up.

"Come on, don't act like that." He came over to her, putting a hand on her shoulder.

"Like what? You've obviously made up your mind." She tossed the laptop aside, staring defiantly up at him. But seeing the fatherly concern in his eyes, she knew he could break her if he wanted to.

"Grace, we're not *forcing* you to go to college. It's just that music's unpredictable. You know that." He peered hopefully at her. "We just want what's best for you, sweetie."

"Fine. I'll go! Are we done?" She just wanted this conversation to end. Besides, she knew she'd been acting childish and selfish. She didn't even like being like this. She reached for her guitar, trying to avoid his gaze. He'd won, right? Why couldn't he just leave? Let her stew in her wimpy compromise for awhile. But instead he reached into his pocket and pulled out what looked like a small jewelry box. What now?

"I know your birthday was last week," he said apologetically. "I don't know if it's the right time, or if any time's right anymore, but it just arrived." He set the box on her desk then stepped back.

"What?" She laid her guitar aside and went over to her desk. What was going on here? Feeling hopeful and expectant, she opened the velvet box and was surprised to see that it contained a pretty silver ring. Suddenly she felt totally off guard by this gift—not to mention ashamed for how she'd acted like such an entitled brat today.

"Thanks," she murmured as she pulled out the ring. But even as the word passed over her lips, it hit her. This was not just an ordinary ring—not just a belated birthday gift. No, of course not.

*This was a promise ring.* The kind of jewelry that dads bestow upon their daughters to ensure that their precious girls do not engage in premarital sex. But something was wrong here. Dads usually did this when their daughters were in, like, middle school. She wasn't even in high school anymore. What was up with this now? She gave him a seriously perplexed expression. *Really?*

"It's called a—"

"I know what it's called, Dad."

"I probably should've done it years ago, but . . ."

She stared down at the ring, trying to imagine that she was thirteen years old and over the moon at this thoughtful fatherly gift. But somehow she just couldn't muster it. Not at this stage of the game. Not after a day when it had felt like all he wanted to do was control her. Why did he not get this?

"So," she started slowly, "now that I'm eighteen you think I'm gonna start sleeping around or something?" She studied him closely.

"Of course not. It's just—"

"Dad, I know what I'm supposed to do or *not* supposed to do. I don't need a ring to remind me." She put the ring back in the box, snapped it closed, and set it back on her desk. Folding her arms across her chest, she stepped away as if the ring was poison and, staring at the floor, she waited for him to leave.

"Grace, what is the matter with you?" he demanded. "Every time we talk lately, everything I say, it's a battle. Would you please look at me?"

With arms still folded in front of her, she glared at him, not saying a word.

"Like at church," he continued hotly, "when I want you on piano, you insist on playing guitar. Or when we rehearse a certain way, and I tell you that's how we're going to play it, and then you still do your own thing."

"I have my own style."

"It was a Chris Tomlin song. It's *worship*. It's not a Renae Taylor concert!"

"Like you know anything about Renae Taylor," she snapped.

"I know she's a bad influence, and her lyrics should make you sick."

"Fans love Renae's lyrics. They love how she sings." She narrowed her eyes. "And some people love how I sing too. Even at church!"

"Grace," he said firmly. "Whether you like it or not, I'm in charge of the band, and you're either part of the team or you're not!"

She sat back on her bed, picking up her laptop. Why was he being so bullheaded? And why didn't he just leave?

"Listen," his tone softened. "I really didn't come in here to fight. We're just concerned about you."

"I'm fine!" she said stubbornly.

Now he just stood there for a long moment, watching her as if he was trying to come up with something intelligent and fatherly to say. Apparently, he was feeling just as blank as she was. Then he picked up the box holding the ring. "If nothing else, just think of the ring as . . . something to remind you how much we love you. You don't have to wear it." Then he left.

Leave it to Dad to get the last word like that. Sure, she knew they loved her. How could she ever forget that? If only they could simply trust her a little more. If only they could let her live her own life and pursue her own dreams. If not now, when she was young and energetic and passionate about music, when?

# Chapter 2

**G**race got up early on Monday morning. Her plan was to write a song. Not just any song but a worship song. And hopefully a really good one. Somehow she felt that if she could successfully do this it might prove to her parents—or maybe to herself—that she really was ready to pursue a career in music. But after a couple of fruitless hours, she felt completely uninspired. Not only that, she felt like climbing the wall.

Deciding that she needed some wide-open spaces to inspire creativity, she packed her guitar into the car and headed off to Homewood City Park. Except for a couple of moms and a handful of kids in the play area, the park was quiet. Grace went over to her favorite bench by the pond and sat down and opened up her guitar case. She removed her guitar and song notebook and took in a slow, deep breath. Much better. She played the chords she'd been toying with, humming along, and hoping that the song would meld together.

But, just like at home, she felt empty and blank. She knew the tune she was playing with had potential. But she felt stuck. Like there was something blocking her. *Just let it flow*, she told herself, *don't hold back*. And so she began stringing along words and rhymes, but the results were so corny and cliché that she could barely stand to hear it. Where was the metaphor she was searching for? Where was the magic?

Finally she realized her efforts were worse than futile; they were downright depressing. And if her music was bumming her, how would it manage to encourage anyone? She looked down at the Fender guitar in her lap, scowling as if it was personally to blame for her complete lack of talent. Okay, that was ridiculous and unfair. She ran her hand over the smooth, wood-grain surface. She loved this nicely worn instrument, knowing it was full of character. She always had loved it—right from the day her father had presented it to her. Unlike the ring he'd given her last night, the guitar was a perfect gift. She still remembered her eighth birthday like it was yesterday.

Her parents had been acting mysterious all morning that day ten years ago. Dad had even pretended to have forgotten it was her birthday altogether, and Mom just kept slipping these sly little glances to Dad. Finally, just when Grace was starting to worry that they truly had forgotten her special day, Dad told her to close her eyes. "No peeking," he said as he turned her round and round. "Now you have to find your gifts yourself."

Her parents chuckled as Grace kept her eyes shut and held out her hands, slowly moving forward.

"Cold, cold," her mom had warned.

So she turned a different direction, shuffling forward.

"You're getting warmer," Dad told her.

"Really warm," Mom added.

"Can I open 'em now?"

"Keep 'em closed." Mom giggled.

"Here," Dad said, "I'll film this."

"No," Mom told him. "I got it. I want you in it with her."

"Red hot!" Dad yelled as Grace's hands touched the couch.

"*Now?*" she eagerly asked them. "Can I open my eyes?"

"Not yet," Dad said. "You ready, Michelle? Getting all this on film for posterity?"

"Yeah."

"All right," Dad told Grace. "Open 'em."

Grace opened her eyes to see the most beautiful guitar in the world. Glowing and golden, it was resting in its opened case that was leaned up against the couch. She could hardly believe her eyes.

"No way!" she said to her parents. Was it really hers?

"You been rockin' on mine," Dad chuckled. "Time you had your own."

"Oh! My! Goodness!" She reached out to touch the sleek surface of the wood, tentatively plucking the strings, which were tuned perfectly. This was really hers!

"You're still great on piano," Dad told her, "but happy birthday, baby."

She looked at Mom, who was giggling as she caught all this on the camcorder. "Well, go ahead," Mom told her. "Play us something."

Happy to accommodate them, Grace picked up the beautiful golden guitar and sat down on the couch, starting to play the chords Dad had taught her on his guitar. Before long, with Mom still running the camcorder, Dad joined her with his guitar, and they began playing "It Is Well" together. And it was really great. But then Grace started to speed up the song, playing louder and harder and imagining she was a real rock star playing for a crowd of fans. And that was when her dad put the brakes on.

"No, no, keep it slow," he said quietly.

"It's better faster," she insisted.

"It's better slow," he gently told her. "It's a slow sort of song."

Grace hadn't agreed with him then anymore than she'd agreed with him yesterday. But grateful for the gorgeous guitar and aware that the camera had still been running, Grace had forced a smile and continued to play—this time more slowly.

Grace sighed as she put her guitar back in its well-worn guitar case. Maybe today wasn't a good day for songwriting after all. Besides, there was something to be said about timing, and if the inspiration wasn't coming, why force it?

Still, as she walked back to the car, she couldn't help but think this was all related to her father. He was always trying to slow her down, always putting on the brakes when she was ready to fly. He seemed to want to mold her and her music into what he considered "good." As if, left to her own devices, she would most certainly drive it straight into the nearest ditch.

As she drove down Main Street, it was becoming clearer and clearer. Whether it was her music or her education or what kind of ring she wore on which finger, Dad wanted his say. And as she parked in front of the bookstore, it was obvious—her dad simply wanted to control her.

Grace went inside the familiar Christian bookstore, where as usual, she was greeted by pleasant inspirational music. She wandered the aisles, checking out the recent releases in the CD section and pausing to admire some of the slick posters of some of the hottest Christian musicians. She knew her dad hoped to see his poster up there someday in the not-so-distant future. And maybe it would happen. It was possible that Johnny Trey's new Christian album would become a massive hit. After all, miracles still happened, didn't they? And even though Grace wasn't a huge fan of her own father's music, there had to be some people out there who were willing to plunk down their hard-earned money to buy his songs. At least the good people of Homewood Community Church should want a Johnny Trey album.

Grace continued wandering, eventually discovering Rachel near the back of the store in the vacation Bible school section. "What's up back here?" Grace asked.

"There's been a run on these materials lately," Rachel explained as she removed some books from a cart.

"Well, it is summer," Grace said in a grumpy tone. "Remember how we always got forced to go to VBS every summer?"

"What's wrong with you?" Rachel gave Grace a curious glance as she slid a workbook onto the shelf.

"Just starting to figure things out." Then, as Rachel filled shelves, Grace quickly told her about this morning's revelation. "It's like Dad wants to control me."

"Your dad just loves you." Rachel studied the spine of a thick book. "You know that."

Now Grace explained it more thoroughly to her. She expounded on the music and college; and, as embarrassing as it was, she even told her about the silly promise ring. "And I am, like, eighteen—*excuse me?*"

Rachel giggled. "That's pretty funny. But I still don't know what you're complaining about."

Grace stared at her friend. Was she serious? Or had she simply gone deaf?

"Grace, your dad's cool." Rachel reached for a small stack of paperbacks.

"See, everyone thinks because he's this 'rock star who got saved,' that makes him cool. Trust me, he's NOT COOL."

Rachel put a finger to her lips. "Hey, keep it down."

Grace exhaled through her nostrils. Why was Rachel being so dense?

"I don't get it," Rachel said gently. "You guys used to be so close. You've been playing together since you were, like six."

"I know. And he still treats me like I'm six!" Grace lowered her voice. "He's *always* in my face. And it's like every second has to turn into this *brilliant* teaching moment."

"All dads do that." Rachel reached for more books.

"Not like mine. He's obsessed."

"Grace, you have the best life ever."

"No. I don't." Grace studied her best friend as she worked. How was it possible that Rachel was siding with Dad?

Rachel stood up straight and looked Grace right in the eye. "Look at you," she said quietly. "You're drop-dead gorgeous. You're this amazing singer. Now, you get to make an album—"

"Dad's album! Don't you get this? It's all *his* songs—played *his* way."

"Well, it is his album, isn't it?"

Grace nodded. "And I get that. I know it's his first album in, like, forever. But still. I mean, seriously, he would never think about doing one of my songs."

"You don't have any songs."

"That's my point!" Grace remembered how hard she'd tried to write a song this morning. It was like Dad had been right there the whole while, breathing down her neck and second-guessing every word, every line, every chord.

Rachel looked confused. "Oh . . . ?"

"I'm *trying* to write," Grace said desperately. "More than anything, I want to write the perfect song so he can't say no. And it's in my head but I can't get it out because . . ." She sighed. "Because he suffocates me."

"Is it really that bad?"

"Yes. And I'm sorry, but I don't want to be the sidekick of the great *one-hit-wonder Johnny Trey* for the rest of my life. I mean, for once, I want to do things my way."

"Okay, I get it." Rachel reached for some workbooks, putting them in numerical order. "But it is worship, right? It's not supposed to be about you, Grace."

Grace just stared at Rachel. Okay, she was right on some levels. But at the same time, why didn't she understand what Grace was trying to tell her? Why was she acting just like Dad? "Yeah, I get that," Grace mumbled. "I know it's worship. What I mean is . . ." She tried to think of a way to make this clear. But the words, just like when she'd been trying to write a song, were stuck inside of her. "Never mind, Rachel. Just forget it." And without saying another word, Grace just walked away. She couldn't get out of the stuffy store quickly enough. Really, why had she even tried to make Rachel understand this? Oh, yeah, because Rachel was supposed to be her best friend. But if her best friend didn't get this, who could?

# Chapter 3

Hey, Johnny," Michelle called out from where she was rinsing something in the sink. "Tim and Sharon are just pulling into the driveway."

"Is it already six?" Johnny set his guitar down on the breakfast nook where he'd been working on a song and slowly stood.

"It's past six," she told him. "Can you go let them in?"

"On my way, darlin'." As he strolled through the dining room, he checked out the nicely laid table. It was great knowing his wife was such a natural hostess. Whether they were entertaining big-wig record moguls or just the neighbors, Michelle always knew exactly what to do and how to do it. Tonight they were having Pastor Tim and his wife, Sharon, for dinner, and the table looked inviting.

"Hello," he said as he opened the door wide. "Welcome, welcome!"

They were barely inside when Michelle joined them, and the four exchanged hugs all around. "I have iced tea and strawberry lemonade in the kitchen," she announced. Soon they all had drinks in hand, and while the women remained in the kitchen, Johnny led Tim to his study, giving him the two-bit tour.

"Aha," Tim said, "so is this where you keep all your music memorabilia." He began scanning the photos and awards displayed on the walls. "Impressive."

Johnny laughed. "Not that impressive. Don't forget it was just one hit."

"But didn't I hear that you're planning to make a new album?"

"That's the plan," Johnny said. "Nothing's written in stone yet."

Tim peered up at a photo of Johnny with some of his recording buddies in Nashville. "Those are some big-name musicians there with you, Johnny."

Johnny nodded. "Yep. At the time we all thought I was going to be a big name too."

"You are a big name," Tim assured him.

"Ah, well, as long as God knows my name." He waved his hand toward the wall behind him. "Believe me, this is all Michelle's doing. She thinks I should have this stuff out for everyone to see. Fortunately we keep it contained to just one room." Johnny tipped his head to the door. "Sounds like Michelle's calling us to dinner now."

"So did you and Michelle live in Nashville?" Tim asked as they walked back through the house.

"Nah. We never actually lived there. But I did grow up ten minutes from Graceland," Johnny said as they went into the dining room where Michelle was telling them were to sit at the table.

Tim chuckled. "Now I get it. That makes sense."

"Yeah, my parents wanted Hank Williams. I gave them Elvis."

The others laughed, and Johnny noticed that Grace's chair was empty. He glanced at Michelle, but she was distracted with filling water glasses.

"I loved Elvis," Sharon said as she sat down.

"Yeah, he was just enough gospel for my parents not to worry about me too much—not at first anyway."

Now Tim pointed to his wife. "*You* loved Elvis?"

This caused even more laughter. But Johnny was distracted by seeing Grace coming into the dining room with her guitar case and Bible in hand. "You going to youth group early tonight?" he asked her.

"Yep." She looked at Michelle. "Sorry you set a plate for me, Mom." She turned to smile at the Bryants. "Nice seeing you guys tonight."

"You too, Grace," Sharon said warmly.

"Have a good evening," Tim told her.

"Hey, Grace," Johnny said as she was going. "Can you fill the car up?"

"Sure."

"You can use the card," he said.

"Okay." She was backing out of the room, obviously eager to be on her way, which made him curious. Why was she in such a hurry, and why was she going early?

"Now don't forget," he warned her.

"I *won't*." Her tone had changed from friendly to crisply irritated.

"Actually, why don't you do it before youth group, Grace?" he added. "So you don't forget."

Now Grace gave him a look to assure him that she was mad or embarrassed or something, but not wanting to put a damper on the evening, he just laughed it off. "Teenagers," he said when he heard the front door slam closed. Fortunately, the Bryants seemed unfazed by his rude daughter. But after the blessing was said, he turned to Tim. "Your kids ever act like that?"

Tim laughed. "Come on, man, I'm a pastor. My kids were perfect."

"That's funny." Sharon shook her head.

Johnny sighed as he shook out his napkin and laid it in his lap. "I don't know what's going on lately. She and I used to be so tight, you know." Now he looked at his guests and made a forced smile. "Glad you wrote a book about this stuff," he said to Tim. "Maybe someday she'll read it."

As food was passed around, Johnny tried to shake off his concerns over his willful daughter. After all, she was still a teenager. They were supposed to go through stages of rebellion, independence, and autonomy. All kids acted out at times. Besides, he reassured himself, Grace was a good Christian girl. And on her way to youth group. Really, what more could a dad wish for?

Grace parked the car on the perimeter of the parking lot, but instead of getting out and going inside, she just sat there thinking. Why was she so angry at her dad? She knew he loved her and, like Rachel kept saying, he really was a good dad. But maybe that was the problem. He was too good of a dad. How often had she heard him joking with his friends, saying things like, "Sure, Grace can date . . . when she's thirty." And, yeah, everyone always laughed, and no one really took him seriously. But sometimes she wondered. Sometimes she felt like if Johnny Trey could have his way, Grace would be a puppet and he would be pulling the strings.

As she got out of the car, she frowned at her innocent-looking guitar and Bible still laying in the backseat. Then she closed the door and locked the car, leaving her guilt alongside the props she had used to slip under Dad's radar tonight. And snuffing out her conscience with angry indignation, she headed toward the entrance of the movie theater, taking her place in line with other young people as she waited to purchase a ticket to a film she knew her parents would never approve of her seeing.

Several acquaintances acknowledged her, but they weren't what she considered close friends. Certainly not anyone from her church, so the chances of them reporting back to her parents was minimal. Not that she particularly cared, or so she told herself as she bought popcorn and soda.

She found a seat down near the front and, feeling a little awkward about being alone, she sat down and began munching on her popcorn. Before long the movie trailers started to play, and all thoughts of parents and youth group and college and life in general were erased by the noise and the music and the action on the big screen in front of her.

When the movie ended, Grace remained in her seat as the credits rolled. It wasn't that she cared who'd been a grip or an assistant-assistant to an assistant producer, but the music kept her there. As she tapped her toes to the beat of a mind-numbing rocker song, she wondered if she would ever get the chance to play like that.

Finally the song and the credits ended and, feeling slightly self-conscious as the house lights came on, she exited the nearly empty theater. Something about this whole scene—church girl sneaking out to watch a questionable flick—seemed sad and pathetic as she walked back to the car. But instead of dwelling on this, she tuned the radio to a rock station and sang loudly along as she took the long way home, arriving at the usual time for a youth group night. Judging by the empty driveway, the Bryants had gone home.

When she reached the door, she realized she'd left her guitar in the car, and not wanting it to sit out in the damp night air, she hurried back to retrieve it. When she came into the house, her mom was straightening the living room.

"Hey," she smiled at Grace. "How was youth group?"

"Fine." Grace noticed her dad over in his favorite chair, seemingly absorbed by something on his laptop. Even so, she suspected he was listening. "It was good," she added for convincing sake as she dropped the car keys in the usual bowl by the front door.

"Did you eat anything?" Mom asked just like she always did after youth group.

"Yeah." Grace was headed for her bedroom now, but apparently Mom was in a chatty mood because she seemed intent on keeping their conversation going.

"I saw Rachel's mom at the gym today," she said lightly. "She was telling me how Rachel is starting at Monroe this fall too."

Grace tightened her grip on the handle of her guitar case as the word *too* grated over her, but she was determined not to show her aggravation.

"Anyway, it sounds like Rachel got some kind of scholarship?"

Grace simply nodded, controlling herself from saying something snarky like, "Yeah, I know. Rachel is perfect. Unlike your loser daughter."

"Rachel's mom said the classes are all listed on their website. That's nice and handy, isn't it?"

Grace nodded again. "Uh-huh." She glanced over at Dad again, but he still seemed intent on his computer, which was odd because he usually had little tolerance for people who allowed their electronic devices to replace good manners. But apparently the rules were different for him.

"So, whenever you want, Grace, you could just go online and start, you know, selecting classes for fall."

"Cool." Grace forced a smile. "I'm gonna go crash now."

"Good-night, sweetie." Her mom looked over at Dad like she'd noticed his lack of social etiquette as well.

"Good-night," Grace said as she headed out.

"You fill the car up?" her dad asked without even looking up from his laptop.

Grace froze in place. Oh, man, how could she have forgotten that? Especially when she'd been trying to be so careful tonight. She watched as her dad reached for his glass of water, taking a long,slow sip with his eyes locked on her, looking at her like he knew. But how could he know? Was her face that easy to read?

"Dad, as soon as I got in the car, Paige called," she began quickly. "And she was crying hysterically and she just really needed to talk. And, well, I guess I completely forgot. I'll go do it now. Okay?"

"Nope." He shook his head in a dismal way as he slowly stood, then walked resolutely to the door.

"I'm sorry, but—"

"*Never mind*." He snatched the keys out of the bowl and stormed out the door, closing it a bit too firmly behind him.

"See what I'm talking about?" she said to Mom.

"Grace." Mom looked intently at her. "This is on you. You said you'd do it, but you broke your word. Again."

Grace just shook her head. It figured that Mom would side with him.

"Look, maybe your father doesn't always show it the way you want, but he loves you so much. Why can't you see that?"

Grace took in a deep breath, considering her response. And then she simply shrugged, turning to go to her room. Really, what was the point of arguing with either of them? They saw things the way they saw them. She was never going to change that.

She quietly closed the door to her room and, for the first time ever, longed for a lock on her door. Not that she wanted to do anything forbidden behind closed doors but mostly to create a barrier between herself and them. She wanted her space!

Fortunately her headphones provided her with a sense of space, even if it was more of an illusion than reality. Just the same, she slipped them into place and opened up her laptop, going directly to the Sapphire Music website. Sapphire was Renae Taylor's label and one of the hottest in the industry. Clicking onto one of Renae's most popular videos, Grace decided to lose herself in the music for awhile. She was just getting into it when she heard someone knocking on her door. Suppressing the urge to yell, "Leave me alone," she tugged off the headphones and said, "Come in," with all the enthusiasm she felt—none.

As Dad entered the room, she closed out Sapphire's website and shut her computer, staring blankly up at him. She knew the aggravation written all over his face was there because of her. She was such a disappointment to him—and all because she'd forgotten to fill up the tank. Seriously, was it that big of a deal?

He held her Bible out to her. "You left this in the car."

"Oh." She reached for it, setting it on the desk next to her. "Thanks."

Dad stepped back to the door but then stopped. With a perplexed expression he rubbed his hand through his hair. He only did this when something was really frustrating him. Something like her.

"You have something you want to tell me?" he asked quietly.

"What?" She frowned. "No."

He let out a long, irritated sigh. "Nothing? Nothing at all?"

"Okay. I'm sorry. I didn't put gas in the car. I'm the worst person ever."

"That's not what I'm talking about," he said sharply.

"Then what?" With defiance in her eyes, she met his stare head on. "Unbelievable! I don't fill the car up, and you come in here and look at me like I'm a serial killer."

Now Dad reached into his shirt pocket and slowly extracted a small slip of paper and set it on her Bible. *Her movie ticket.* She took in a sharp breath, trying to think of some way out of this, but she knew it was futile. He knew. "How was the movie?" he asked in a flat tone. She couldn't even look at him.

"This pattern, Grace. *These lies!*"

She looked up now, locking eyes with him again, bracing herself for what she knew was coming.

"And your attitude!" He grimly shook his head. "You *know* it's a sin to lie. What on earth are you thinking?"

She just continued staring at him. If he thought he was a perfect picture of Christ, he really needed to take another look.

"Are you?" he demanded.

"Am I what?"

*"Thinking!"* His features twisted in anger. "Are you even thinking, Grace? Because none of this makes any sense to me. You *never* used to be this way."

She looked back down at her Bible and the theater ticket. As much as she knew what she'd done was wrong, what about how he was acting right now? Was it right to stand there and make your daughter feel like dirt? She could feel tears building in her eyes, but she was determined not to cry. No, she was going to take this like an adult. Because, whether Dad believed it or not, she was an adult. And maybe if he would quit treating her like a child, she would have a chance to act like one.

"Grace, I know you've always wanted your life to be about God. But lately you're just all about *you*."

She took in a deep breath. Did he really believe that?

"I've always told you we'd be a team, but if this doesn't stop, I don't see how you can stay in the worship band . . . or be part of the album."

She slowly exhaled, calculating his words, his intent. Now she forced what she hoped was an apologetic expression. "I'm sorry, Dad."

He pursed his lips and shook his head. "It's late. We have church in the morning. Since I haven't replaced you on the worship team yet, I'll expect you to do your part. *On piano.*" He pointed his finger at her. "Don't let me down."

He shook his head again as he reached for the door. His disappointment in her was so intense, so palpable, she could still feel it in the air after he left. And maybe she did deserve his scorn and criticism. Maybe she was a disappointment to God as well. However, as she got ready for bed, she was determined to do better tomorrow. Somehow she was going to change Dad's perception of her. Somehow she was going to make him proud of her.

# Chapter 4

Resolved to make her father happy today, Grace took her place on the stage and put her best effort into the first worship song. She liked "Desert Song" well enough, but she knew her heart was not fully engaged. Still she was determined not to disappoint.

As she played along with the other worship leaders, singing the familiar song with as much enthusiasm as she could muster, she observed a well-dressed man slipping into the back of the church—at least ten minutes late. As he made his way up the aisle, taking a seat about midway up, she could see that he appeared to be a little older than her dad and, as far as she could tell, a newcomer to the church. But it was his slick *GQ* appearance that captured her attention. Her guess was that he wasn't from Homewood.

As the song ended, she focused her attention back on Dad, waiting for him to cue her to begin the next song. She continued to put her energy into playing and singing the worship songs—playing the part of the worship leader's well-mannered daughter. She would make him happy, make him proud. She would give her best efforts, and maybe he would start to trust her again.

After the worship ended, Pastor Bryant came up and took over the podium, and Grace went to sit where she usually sat, on the left-hand side of the front row. And there she pretended to be taking notes, but she was actually writing down some song lyrics that had just hit her. Then aware that her dad was probably watching, she tried to remember to open her Bible at the appropriate times. Before long the sermon ended, and it was time for the worship team to wrap things up.

Once again she took her place at the piano and did her best to make Dad happy. Sure, it wasn't how she would be running the show if she were in charge. But she was not in charge. Not of the worship service—and not even of her own life.

Relieved that it was all over, Grace kept a pleasant expression pasted on her face as she gathered her music and notebook and Bible, shoving them into her oversized bag and preparing to make a quick exit. Dad gave her a subtle nod—as if to say she'd done okay—and then he turned to pack up his guitar. She was just leaving the stage when she heard someone calling out, "Johnny Trey!"

She looked over to see the *GQ* stranger approaching the stage, waving at her dad like he knew him.

"*Mossy?*" Her dad sounded genuinely shocked.

"In the flesh, amigo." The man came up to the stage with a look of quiet self-assurance and confidence—like he really knew who he was and could fit in anywhere, even a small church in Alabama.

"Come here, man!" Dad hopped off the stage and met the stranger with a big hug. "Dude, what in the world?"

"Let me look at you." Mr. *GQ* gave Dad a quick head-to-toe then shook his head. "Man, you're old."

Now Mom was coming over to check the situation out. She looked as curious as Grace felt. *"Mossy?"* Mom said with uncertainty as she got closer.

"There she is," the man said warmly to her. "Shelly, baby." Now he hugged Mom too. Grace, remaining in the shadows, continued watching, trying to figure out who this was and what was going down.

"You haven't aged a day, sweet thing," Mr. *GQ* was telling her mom.

"I'll take your word for it," she said happily.

"What are you *possibly* doing here, man?" Dad asked him.

Now Mr. *GQ* nodded to where Grace was standing nearby eavesdropping. "Who's this young talent?" he asked her dad.

"That's Grace," Dad told him.

Mr. *GQ* looked stunned. *"What?"*

"Our daughter," Mom explained. "Come here, Grace. Meet an old friend."

"This beautiful lady is baby Grace?" He extended his hand for a shake then pulled Grace into a warm hug. "Last time I saw you, you were in diapers."

"Grace," Dad said to her, "this is Frank Mostin. He was my manager." He chuckled. "He discovered your old man back in the day."

"Hi." Grace smiled shyly at him.

"You are absolutely gorgeous." Now Mossy gave her the same head-to-toe he'd given Dad, only this time he looked pleased. "And you were brilliant up there." He nodded to the stage. "A real natural."

With a grimace Grace shrugged then thanked him. Did this guy really think *that* was good? Compared to how she wished she could play, today's worship service was nothing. Then, realizing this dude was really studying her, she started to feel uncomfortable.

"Alright," Dad said. "You completely got me. What brings you out this way, man?"

"Well, I'm just so happy to see you both. I've missed you, and I mean that." He patted Dad on the back. "And I have some exciting news. Is there somewhere we can talk?"

Mom invited Mossy to come to their house, and Dad gave him directions. Before long they were driving home, and today the talk in the front seat was not the usual rehash of what happened in church. Today the talk was all around Mossy. Speculating why he was here, what kind of news he had, and reminiscing over back when Dad and Mossy were working together. It was impossible to miss the excitement in Dad's voice as he talked about the "good old days."

Mom recruited Grace to help her get lunch ready, and soon they were all gathered at the eating nook together, where the conversation, like in the car, seemed stuck in a time gone by. Even so, Grace listened with interest. It was actually amusing to hear Mossy talking about Dad in his younger days, making him seem almost human. Although her dad shut Mossy down on a couple of wild-sounding tales. Probably because his daughter was listening.

Dad and Mossy continued chattering happily as Grace and Mom cleared the table. "I can finish this up," Mom told her. "I'm sure you have other things you'd rather be doing, sweetie."

Grace actually wanted to stick around and continue listening in on what seemed a fairly intriguing conversation. Then spotting Mom's laptop on the kitchen desk, Grace thought of a good excuse. "Hey, did you look up the Monroe website yet?" she asked, nodding to the computer.

Mom smiled. "As a matter of fact, I did." She hurried over and opened the lid. "I happen to have it right here. Would you like to take a peek?"

"Sure." Grace sat down at the breakfast bar with the laptop, pretending to peruse the site, although she was actually listening in to conversation going on in the nearby nook.

"Yeah," Dad was saying. "We would travel to churches all over. And I'd share my story and—"

"Wait," Mossy stopped him. "You mean you made a living going to churches and telling your story?"

"Did it for years." Dad told him. "Grace and I would play. I'd speak. Just moved here a couple of years ago."

"So what you did today, that's your job now?"

"Yeah. Music pastor. We're also prepping for an album. I've written some songs, so . . . we'll see."

"Religious songs?" Mossy sounded doubtful.

"Worship songs, yeah. . . . But hey, man, you didn't come all this way to hear my story."

"No, it's good to hear. Actually it plays into why I came. I mean the fact that you're still playing and writing and everything. You remember Larry Reynolds?"

"Sure."

"Don't know if you heard, but a few months ago he was named president of Sapphire Music."

Grace looked up from the screen with interest. Sapphire was Renae's label.

"Nice." Dad nodded.

"Yeah. So I pay my old friend a visit, congratulate him, and everything. And you know the first thing he says? He starts talking to me about *American Idol*, Sweden."

Grace could see that Dad wasn't following this—what happens when you live under a stone.

"You don't know?" Mossy looked surprised.

Dad just shrugged.

"You are out of it." Mossy laughed. "Some Swedish kid sang 'Misunderstood' on *Idol* and won the whole thing. After that, the video went viral."

"What video?" Dad frowned.

"Yours! The live one, from the Greek. Couple hundred thousand hits."

"Wow!" Dad looked impressed.

"Yeah, I guess everything comes back in style, doesn't it? Anyway, Larry and I go out for drinks. Before you know it, he gives me an office in the Sapphire building."

"That's great, man." Dad slapped Mossy on the back. "Congrats."

"Yeah, it's great when friends help friends. But that's not the best part. You ready?" Mossy's eyes were glinting with excitement. "He and I worked it out. Sapphire Music wants to offer you a deal."

Grace was so stunned she almost fell off the stool. Dad was being offered a recording contract with Sapphire Music? Was this for real?

"Just a one-off for now, but I got him to commit, in advance, to a full domestic tour to support the new album! As far as the songs, it's hands-off. Write whatever you want. Not religious stuff, of course, but he said as long as you sing 'Misunderstood' on tour, the rest is your call."

"Wow. That's . . ." Dad rubbed his chin. "That's really humbling."

"It's huge!" Mossy assured him. "And I don't need to tell you these deals don't come easily. Johnny, we're back in the game!"

"Sounds like an incredible opportunity—"

"Thank you! I worked hard for it."

"I appreciate that, man, I really do." Dad sighed. "But I'm gonna pass, Moss."

"What?" Mossy's expression was a mix of hurt and disbelief.

"Hey man, I'm sorry you made the long trip and everything. I mean, it's great to see you, but it's not my thing anymore, you know?"

"Not your thing?" Mossy frowned. "Johnny, you got your life back in order. You're looking good. There's no passing on this!"

"I get it. I do. Just . . . it's not me anymore. I like what I'm doing now."

The room was quiet now, and Grace was controlling herself from jumping up and down and demanding to know why Dad wanted to take a pass on an offer like this. What was wrong with the man?

"So . . . uh," Mossy nodded over to where Mom was still puttering in the kitchen and Grace was supposedly studying the Monroe website.

"It's alright," Dad assured him. "Say whatever you want."

There was another long pause. Then Mossy started talking again, more quietly this time. "Remember when you were playing bars at airports or any coffeehouse with an open mic? Who gave you your shot?"

"Moss, we had a great run—"

"Or when you were passed out drunk or the time you woke up behind bars. Who was there for you?"

Grace saw her dad glancing her direction, as if he wasn't sure he wanted her to hear this. But she just pretended to be absorbed by the boring college site.

"You did a ton for me, Moss. That's why I gave you my song. I want to help you out, man—"

"Then do this!"

Grace's head popped up, and she watched openly as her dad slowly shook his head. "No."

"Johnny . . ."

"Come on, Moss, if 'Misunderstood' is hot again, go ahead and do a remake. You own it."

"Get that kid from *Idol*—"

"Johnny, he wants you!"

"Look, tell Larry thanks, but—"

"Listen, I know this is all very sudden. Take some time. You and Shelly think it over."

Dad just shook his head again. "I'm sorry, Moss. My mind is made up."

Mossy stood now. Grace could tell he was not the least bit pleased with her dad's answer, but he smiled just the same. And thanking them for lunch, he went on his way.

The room grew quiet as Mom poured soap in the dishwasher, shut the door, and turned it on. Grace, tired of feigning interest in a college she never wanted to attend, quietly closed the laptop. And without saying a word to either of her parents, she headed off to her room.

She immediately went for her headphones and her computer, and before long, she was listening to her dad's one hit song—"Misunderstood." As she listened, she Googled Frank Mostin Management, pulling up Mossy's website. She clicked on his bio, browsing through old photos until she found one of Mossy and her dad. Together they were grinning and holding up a gold record. The caption read: *Frank Mostin with Johnny Trey celebrating their top-ten hit, "Misunderstood."*

Before the song ended, she pulled off her headphones and tossed them onto her bed. How could her dad be so stupid? To throw away an opportunity like that? What was wrong with the man? Or maybe he was just too good. What was that old saying—too heavenly minded to be any earthly good? Yeah, that just about described her dad. The one-hit wonder who was so heavenly minded, so intent on playing only worship songs, that he was practically useless.

# Chapter 5

Johnny wished he could put the whole thing behind him, but as the evening wore on, he continued to feel slightly haunted by Moss's unexpected visit. As if a ghost from his past had come knocking. Although he'd been careful not to mention anything too specific about Mossy to Grace, because he could tell her antennas were up and he suspected that she didn't approve of his decision to send his old buddy packing, he had capitalized on what he hoped was a teachable moment. Because if Grace couldn't glean some things from her old man's experiences, who could? Of course, in typical Grace style, she listened with an expression of skepticism on her face. What was it with eighteen-year-olds these days?

After Grace turned in for the night, probably to escape further lectures, he sat down on the couch and thought about the whole thing with Mossy. He knew he'd been right to do what he'd done, but he did wonder if he might have handled it differently. After all, Moss was an old friend, and Johnny cared about where Mossy might be spending eternity. Perhaps he'd missed an opportunity. And yet, at the same time, the memories of how his own life had been so lost and adrift were unsettling.

It was getting close to eleven when Michelle came in to inquire how Johnny was faring. "You alright?" she asked with concerned eyes. "You seem awfully quiet."

He shrugged. "Just thinking."

"What are you thinking about?" She sat next to him on the couch, pulling her knees up as she snuggled close.

"You know . . . the business with Moss," he explained.

"You regretting your answer?"

"No, no, that's not it at all."

"I'm sure Mossy thought he was making you a tempting offer."

"Yeah, and I can't blame him for trying."

"Didn't turn your head?" she said in good-natured teasing. "Hearing about that *American Idol* kid? Not even a little?"

"I stand by my decision."

"Then why do you seem troubled?"

"Just seeing him again takes me back. You know?"

She nodded, snuggling in closer. "Yeah. Me too."

He wrapped his arm around her, pulling her closer. "And I feel kinda bad for Moss's sake. He seemed so hopeful. I felt like I busted his balloon."

"And rained on his parade," she added a bit glibly.

"Uh-huh." He sighed. "But he'll be alright. Moss is a survivor."

"Yeah."

"It's just that I haven't thought about all that stuff, Michelle. You know, for so long."

"What stuff exactly?" she asked.

"I don't know exactly—just the past in general, I guess." He sighed. "You know I used to talk about everything pretty openly, back when we were doing the church ministry. But getting settled here in Homewood these past few years, it's almost like I lost touch with that part of my life. Like it didn't really happen. You know?"

"Uh-huh."

"Thinking about it all tonight, it just kinda hit me—how I shouldn't even be here." He turned to look into her face. "The drugs alone should've killed me."

"But they didn't." She gave him a sleepy smile. "Because God had different plans for you, Johnny Trey."

He hugged her. "Am I thankful for that."

"Don't worry about Mossy," she said quietly. "He'll land on his feet."

"Uh-huh. He always does."

The next afternoon Grace walked into the bookstore, searching for Rachel. She'd called earlier, explaining how she really needed to talk, and Rachel had offered to take her afternoon break with Grace. "Just as long as you understand I have to be back to work on time," she'd warned. "My break is only twenty minutes, you know."

"Rachel's in the break room," Lindy the cashier told Grace.

"Thanks." Grace hurried to the back of the store, finding Rachel reading a magazine and sipping on a soda. "You started your break without me?" She frowned at her friend.

"Sorry, we take our breaks when we're scheduled to take them." She gave an apologetic smile. "What's up, drama queen?"

Grace resisted the urge to argue this. Instead she launched into yesterday's meeting with Mossy. "I couldn't believe it," she said. "He'd come all this way to see Dad. And he's working for Sapphire Music. You know that's Renae Taylor's record company too. So Mossy informs Dad that his one-hit-wonder 'Misunderstood' is making a serious comeback because some Swedish kid sang it on *Idol* and won."

"A Swedish kid won *American Idol*?" She frowned.

"*American Idol, Sweden*," Grace corrected. "Anyway, he's offering my dad this incredible deal—like on a silver platter—you can record anything you want, man, just sign on the dotted line."

"Uh-huh?" Rachel offered Grace her bag of chips.

Grace waved her hand. "And my dad rejects his offer. Flat out rejects it. Mossy offered to let Dad think it over, but no, Dad says he's certain. He did not want a record deal."

"But why not? I thought your dad was getting ready to do a worship album. Why not just do it with this Mossy character?"

Grace sighed. "Because they don't want religious songs."

"Oh." Rachel nodded with a knowing look. "Well, then I don't blame your dad at all. He made the right choice."

Grace fought back the urge to yell at her best friend. Why was Grace acting like this? Always taking her dad's side? Whose best friend was she anyway?

"I honestly don't see why you're so upset about this, Grace."

Grace honestly did not see why Rachel was being so dense. But somehow she had to make Rachel get it. She had to get Rachel to act like friends were supposed to act—sympathetic, seeing her side of things. "So then Mossy leaves, and my dad launches into this, like, ten-hour speech on *motives* and *temptation* and how the world was so empty for him when he was making music. And he was talking about how everyone has a different calling, and how he's so fulfilled now, and everything. Like it was supposed to be this fabulous teachable moment for me."

"What's wrong with that?"

Grace rolled her eyes. "Nothing! Except that I've heard it, like, a million times. He said it in every single church we ever played at! Sheesh, I was there, okay? And yet my dad acts like I'd never heard it before."

"Oh." Rachel set down her soda can with a thoughtful look. Like maybe she was finally getting it. "You have to admit that it's pretty cool your dad's song is getting so many hits."

Grace just shook her head.

"Sorry." Rachel sounded defensive. "I just think it's kinda cool."

"Whatever."

"I mean 'Misunderstood' was recorded so long ago. And now it's making this great comeback. That's got to feel good."

"What difference does it make?" Grace demanded. "Dad turned them down. He's so lame. Do you know what he told Mossy?"

"Obviously not. I wasn't there, Grace."

"Dad told Mossy that if 'Misunderstood' was so big, Sapphire should just get someone else to do a remake. Can you believe that? He just handed over his one and only big hit. Like he didn't even care."

"What did the guy say?"

Grace's mind was moving down another track now. Suddenly she saw the answer to this dilemma—as if it was written on the sky or at least on a rock concert poster. "Huh?" She looked back at Rachel who seemed to be waiting for some answer.

"What did that Moss guy say when your dad told him to get someone else to record 'Misunderstood'?"

"I don't remember."

Rachel downed the last of her soda then pointed at the clock by the door. "That's just as well since my break time is officially over. See ya!"

Grace kept sitting there in the break room, running a crazy idea around and around inside her head. Who was to say it couldn't happen?

Suddenly Grace remembered that today was Monday. And her parents had their small group tonight, which meant she would have the house to herself, which meant she could make as much noise—rather music—as she pleased. The plan was clicking into place.

Once she got home, she spent some time in her room, getting everything lined up and worked out. She would have between two and three hours tonight—to get it just right. After she felt she'd gotten her ducks lined up—as well as she knew how—she went down to help Mom with dinner. Acting like the perfect daughter, she even chatted with Mom about the classes she might end up taking at Monroe—as if she really planned on going. By the time Dad came home, they appeared to be the perfect little Christian family, all sitting down to a friendly meal together. Little did her parents know, she was just counting the minutes until she would have the house to herself.

"I'll clean up the kitchen," she told Mom when they were finished eating. "That'll give you more time to spruce up for your group thing."

Mom blinked in surprised. "Well, thanks. I'm happy to take you up on that offer."

Dad looked surprised too, but he also looked slightly dubious. "What's up with the good-daughter routine? You getting ready to hit me up with a request for money?"

She gave him a look. "So I try to act in a more mature fashion, and you make fun of me?"

He held up his hands. "No, no, I'm not making fun." He smiled. "In fact, I like this." And before she could show him how exasperating he was, he hurried away. With her parents out of the kitchen, she haphazardly loaded the dishwasher, not even bothering to rinse the dishes like they usually did. Instead, she piled them in, added a generous measure of dishwasher soap, then turned it onto the pots and pans cycle and proceeded to wipe down the countertops and table. She was just finishing up when she heard them calling good-bye, and when she peered out the window, they were getting into the car and pulling out. Just like clockwork.

She threw the dishcloth into the sink, then raced up to her room where her laptop was already propped up, just the right height on a stack of books on her desk. It was all set and ready to record. She took a moment to fluff her hair and apply some fresh lip gloss. Then, satisfied that she looked good, she grabbed her guitar.

Her heart was pounding with excitement as she strapped on her guitar—almost as if she were getting ready to stand before a packed coliseum. But first she wanted to do a little warm-up. She played some chords and ran through some vocals. Finally, confident that she was ready for this, she hit "record" on her laptop. Then, positioning herself on the hot pink Post-it note she'd stuck to her rug earlier, she took in a deep breath and began to belt out a guitar-and-vocal solo she felt certain was about to launch her career in music.

She did several takes before she was satisfied she had a really good one. Even then she watched it four times before she decided that it was perfect—or as near perfect as she could get in her small, impromptu recording studio. And then she pulled up the carefully worded e-mail she'd written and saved as a draft this afternoon, and she attached the song to it and hit "send."

She looked over at the alarm clock by her bed, relieved to see it was only 8:45. She had time to spare. And now she realized, she would be playing the waiting game. How long would it take?

On Tuesday morning Frank Mostin didn't feel the least bit eager to go back to his office. Because Monday had been a travel day, he had scheduled his meeting with Sapphire for Tuesday afternoon. Of course, at the time he'd imagined himself showing up the hero—he would tell the story, embellishing as needed, of how he'd won back Johnny Trey to the music business. It had seemed such a solid plan last week—a real slam dunk—that he'd pushed to have their meeting as soon as possible. And Larry Reynolds had gladly cleared his calendar to accommodate Mossy.

But if Mossy could've delayed the inevitable for another day or two or three or ten, he would've gladly done so. To say he wasn't looking forward to meeting with his friend and president of Sapphire was an understatement. However, as he rode up the elevator to his own office, just a few floors down from Sapphire, he reminded himself that Larry Reynolds was his friend and had been for years. But as the sleek chrome doors slid open, he remembered his old motto—*Friends are friends, but business is business.* And this was business. He had failed to deliver Johnny Trey to Sapphire. Period.

He tipped his head to the receptionist as he passed through the lobby area on his floor. As usual, he kept up his bravado. No one would guess that his mission down south had been unsuccessful. At least not until after the one o'clock meeting at Sapphire. It wouldn't take long for the news to leak out after that. By the time he went home from work today, everyone in the industry would know. And, unless friendship meant more to Larry than money—and Mossy doubted that, Frank Mostin's name would be mud at Sapphire. And everywhere else too.

He went into his office and closed the door. By this time next week, he'd probably have to start working out of his home again. And it wasn't that he didn't like working from home—the commute was a breeze—he knew that clients didn't take him quite as seriously as when he had an office downtown where the action was.

He sighed as he opened his briefcase and removed his laptop. Maybe he was getting too old for this business. Music was for young people, and he'd be sixty in a couple of years. Maybe he should look into something else, like real estate maybe. He was a natural salesman. But the real estate market was still in a slump. Kind of like his life.

As his computer warmed up, he quickly checked his phone messages, flipping through them quickly, holding onto the slimmest hope that Johnny might've changed his mind and called. Of course, he hadn't. Besides, if he was going to call, he would've used the cell phone number on the business card Mossy had given to him. When his computer screen lit up, he decided to check his e-mail too, just in case. Usually he let his assistant sift the posts for him—so much junk to wade through—but still hoping that Johnny might've come through after all, he carefully skimmed down the list.

The name Trey immediately caught his attention, and with trembling hand and a heart full of anticipation, he clicked on the e-mail. To his surprise, it wasn't from Johnny at all. It was from Johnny's pretty blonde daughter. Curious as to why the girl was writing to him, he quickly read the e-mail and was completely floored to learn that she wanted a chance to record her father's one-hit wonder.

"Is it possible?" he said aloud as he grabbed his headphones, anxiously plugging them into the computer and opening her attachment. "Is it even possible?" A huge smile filled his face as he looked at the image of a girl who by all appearances had star quality. But then, when she started to sing, rocking out as she played guitar—and played it extremely well, he burst into laughter. Joyous laughter. "She's got it," he said to himself when he finally removed his headphones. "The little girl's got it." He read her name on the e-mail. "Grace Trey." He shook his head in wonder. "I've been saved by Grace."

By the time he marched into Larry's posh office, Mossy was flying high. Not only did Grace Trey have real star potential; she was even better than her old man. His plan was to play this for Larry like it was his intention from the start. "Johnny Trey is yesterday's news," he announced to Larry and his associates. "The next generation is where it's at. I'd like to introduce you to Grace Trey, Johnny Trey's daughter." Without further ado, Mossy hit "play." And despite the fact that the girl had recorded this song from what appeared to be her own bedroom, the sound quality wasn't too bad, and it took only moments for the Sapphire folks to see that she was really good.

"Good looking too," Larry observed.

"Nice work, Mossy," one of the associates told him.

"When can you get her in here for a recording session?" Larry asked. "The sooner we get that record rereleased, the better it'll be for everyone, and I'm sure you know what I mean."

"Let's go over the contract details first," Mossy told them. And knowing he had them in the palm of his hand, he specified what he felt his client needed, and he wasn't afraid to push them a little. After all, that was his job. Besides, he wanted her to be comfortable and happy. And if this turned into more than a one-song deal, like he hoped, it would pay off. But even if it was just a single, having "Misunderstood" out there in the marketplace again wouldn't hurt his bank account any.

"Can you get her in here by the end of the week—or early next week at the latest?" one of the associates asked.

"You get me an offer," Mossy told them, "and I'll get her in here."

"Good work, Moss." Larry gave him a fist bump as they were wrapping it up. "I'm guessing this'll be way better than just a dusted-off Johnny Trey record. That little girl is marketable—as well as a name. We play it right, and we can make her a star."

As Mossy walked down the hall to the elevators, he admired the sleekly framed music posters adorning the wall. He paused to imagine his new client's pretty face right up there next to Renae Taylor. Heck, if this went the way he hoped it'd go, little Grace might be opening for Ms. Taylor before the year was up.

Now all he had to do was get her signed. And since she was eighteen, he wasn't too worried about Johnny interfering. Well, he was a little worried. But he knew that Grace was hungry for this—he'd seen that look before. Nothing was going to stop that little girl from chasing her dream. He was banking on it.

# Chapter 6

Grace felt like she'd been walking a tightrope these past few days. Carefully gauging each step, guarding her thoughts, watching her words, trying to contain her excitement and trying to figure this thing out. And her behavior had not gone unnoticed by her parents either. Both of them had mentioned together and separately that she seemed more mature and reasonable lately. Oh, if only they knew.

Several times she had almost opened up to them. But each time Dad had blown it by saying something overly protective or judgmental or even joking at her expense. Sure, he was just being Dad, but if he had any idea how many times he'd shut her down, and she'd closed them out. . . . Well, it was probably better this way. This wasn't the kind of thing she could expect them to be reasonable about. She knew her dad too well. And even though Mom would be hurt, she would understand in time.

By Sunday morning Grace knew it was high time to blow the lid off this thing. And she knew just the place to do it—and how. It wasn't that she wanted to hurt her mom or embarrass her dad. She simply wanted him to back off and give her some space. Sometimes the only way to get space was to blast everything apart. Besides, she reassured herself as the band assembled on the stage, getting ready for worship, the congregation would probably appreciate this. Some of them might even thank her later. And it would give them a performance to remember her by.

So the worship began as usual, with everyone in their places just like they'd been at rehearsal, with her dad in front leading them—controlling their every move. And for the opening song, Grace did as she'd been told. But right before the second song began, she picked up her guitar, which she'd stashed behind an amp, and, quickly strapping it on while Dad was encouraging the congregation to really "get into" this next song, she plugged it in. By the time Dad started the song and happened to glance her direction, it was too late. The look on his face was priceless.

Really, Grace told herself, as she *got into it*, this song deserved this kind of attention. And she played and sang like she was rocking it in front of fans. And it seemed like most of the congregation got into it—almost like Dad had invited them to. As she watched their faces, she could see that some were a little uneasy, but the younger ones seemed grateful. As if she'd woken them up and given them a reason to clap and sing and worship God with real enthusiasm. Wasn't that how it was supposed to be done?

She could see behind her Dad's phony smile that he was smoldering as he played. And yet he kept his voice even after the song ended. He even made a joke about the apple not falling far from the tree—his daughter the rock star. The congregation laughed hard about that. Who would have the last laugh?

But as they started the next song, he gave her the look. And since this song really was meant to be a slow and thoughtful song, she toned it down. But she didn't do it for Dad. She did it for the song and for the congregation. However, each time they did a lively song, Grace was back on guitar, singing and playing with abandon.

By the time the service ended, Grace wasn't sure what was going on with Dad. In a way he seemed almost resolved. Like he was maybe giving in to her music and her style. Like maybe he was finally ready to give her a little space to breathe. And as they visited with members of the congregation—and she enjoyed the compliments they were giving her and Dad just smiled and laughed and joked—she started to feel truly hopeful. Dad was really coming around.

Even Pastor Tim caught her as she was going out. "That was surprisingly refreshing," he said. Those were his exact words.

"Thanks, it was all my dad's idea."

As they walked out to the car, waving and greeting friends, Grace thought maybe they'd reached some new milestone in their relationship. Dad was finally cutting the puppet strings, finally letting her grow up and spread her wings musically.

Grace let out a little sigh of relief as Dad calmly started the engine. Mom was making the usual small talk about church and friends and what they would have for lunch today and then—just as the SUV was out on the street and a safe distance away from the church, Dad exploded. "What on earth do you think you were doing in there, Grace Rose Trey?"

"Singing?"

"Don't get smart with me, young lady."

"Dad, I was just—"

"You know you stepped over the line. Way over the line. And you don't even care, do you?"

"Johnny." Mom put her hand on his arm. "Let's keep this calm."

He barely nodded. "Yeah. Right. Calm." He took in a deep breath. "So, tell me, what were you doing in there, Grace?"

"I was just trying to—"

"*Take over.* That's what you wanted to do." He hit his palm against the steering wheel. So much for calm. "You wanted to take over and turn our worship service into the *Grace Trey Concert.* You think the congregation is there to see you—Grace

Trey, the big rock star. You think you're the next Renae Taylor. Don't pretend I'm wrong, Grace. I could see it in your eyes."

"I don't think you can see anything, Dad. Even when it's right in your face."

"Grace!" Mom's voice had the edge of warning in it.

"I'm sorry, Mom," she said angrily. "But it's true. Dad is totally clueless when it comes to me and my music."

"*Your* music?" He slowly shook his head. "When we lead worship, it's God's music, Grace. Don't you get that?"

"I get that it's *your* music, Dad. And anything I want to do differently is wrong. I get it. *All right?*"

"Grace, that's *not* the point, and you know it!

"It was so much better than the boring thing we rehearsed and everybody *loved* it, Dad. Didn't you see them?"

Dad was taking in a big breath now, like he was just getting ready to explode all over again.

"Grace," Mom said gently as she placed her hand on Dad's arm again, her signal for him to calm down. "Dad's right. It's not your call to make. Your dad is the worship leader. It's his job to call the shots."

"I know!" Grace slumped down in the seat, feeling like an eight-year-old again. "He's said it a hundred times already."

Now the car was silent, and Grace knew that her hope that Dad was finally letting her grow up was just an illusion. How could she have been so naïve? No one said anything, and after what seemed an eternity, Dad was finally pulling into their driveway. Grace was about to hop out as they waited for the garage door to go up, but Dad didn't even push the button. "One more thing, Grace." He got out of the car and came around to where she was getting out, looking her directly in the eyes. "How can you explain lying to Pastor Tim?"

"Lying?"

Dad nodded with a grim expression. "About the worship service. Why did you lie to him like that?"

"Come on," Mom was saying as she hurried to the front door. "Let's take this inside."

Grace followed her, trying to remember exactly what she'd said to their pastor when he'd complimented her. Hadn't she tried to give Dad the credit for the worship service? What was wrong with that?

Now they were standing in the entry of their house—a neat little triangle just inside the front door, where neighbors couldn't see them.

Dad looked her in the eyes again, like he was trying to pry some lame confession from her. "Don't tell me you didn't do it, Grace. I was coming up right behind you, standing behind the door as you were talking. You told Pastor Tim it was *my* idea for you to switch tempo."

"You were spying on me?" Now she felt outraged. When had her dad turned into such a dictator?

"No! I wasn't spying on you. I was—"

"Why don't you put one of those ankle things on me too! That way you can track me 24–7!"

"Don't you dare try to spin it that way! You lied to the pastor's *face*!"

"Yeah! And you used to get drunk and go to jail!" Grace was biting back tears now. But she didn't want Dad to see her crying. Didn't want him to think he'd gotten the best of her.

"You're done," he seethed. "You're out of the band. And you can forget the album too."

She glared at him, wondering how this monster could really be her father. "Good!" she shouted at him. "I don't want to be on your stupid album anyway!"

As she turned to go to her room, she could hear Mom trying to calm him down. Mr. Worship Leader one minute and Monster Dad the next. What would Pastor Tim think if he could see them now?

She turned to look at them, wanting to get one final jab. "You know what, Dad?" she said in a challenging tone. "Even Pastor Tim liked what I did today. But I guess you didn't *spy* on that part, did you?" Now she ran up to her room and slammed the door shut. She was tempted to jam her desk chair under the doorknob like they did in movies, but she knew that was pushing it. Besides it was just a matter of time until she was completely free of these shackles.

Just then her cell phone rang. She looked at the caller ID and saw that it was from Mossy. Could this be it . . . a way out of this town, away from these people who were trying to control her, keep her down? Tentatively she answered the phone.

As Grace packed, she felt seriously regretful about one thing. She would miss Noah Roberts's recital performance tonight. Oh, she knew the nine-year-old would be just fine. Noah was extremely talented on guitar and truly her star student. He would start out feeling nervous—everyone did at that age. But if he'd just remember what she'd told him, he would begin to relax. And then he would play beautifully. She knew it.

She wiped a tear from her cheek as she stuffed the last of her things into the wheeled carry-on bag, zipping it up. She just hoped he would understand why she couldn't be there. And maybe once she got settled she would send him a note of explanation and encouragement. Or not. After all, becoming a star wasn't easy or pain free. If he loved music as much as he claimed, he might as well start learning this lesson now.

# Chapter 7

After a restless night of tossing and turning and little sleep, Johnny got up earlier than usual. Hopefully a good long jog would clear his head. And maybe even settle his heart. He wasn't proud of the way he'd handled Grace yesterday. But his little girl needed to be brought back down to earth. And that was his job, wasn't it? God expected him to raise his daughter to be respectful and obedient. If someone had taught Johnny these things when he was Grace's age, his life might not have gone into the ditch so many times. Man, if only these kids came with an instruction manual.

He could smell the bacon frying even before he came in the front door. Bless that wife of his. She knew just what a man needed after a rough night and hard workout. He headed straight for the kitchen and a drink of water. "Smells mighty good in here," he said as he watched her measuring coffee. "I'd give you a hug, but I'm all sweaty."

"Thanks." She made a grateful smile but her eyes looked troubled. He guessed, like him, she'd had a restless night too. "Good run?"

"Yeah." He set the empty glass on the counter and then glanced at the clock. "She come out yet?"

"No," Michelle studied him as she pressed the button on the coffeemaker. "You okay?"

He let out a long sigh. "Oh, you know, she's been a pain. But I know I was wrong to lose it like that."

She nodded. "Uh-huh."

"I got to make it right."

She nodded again. "I'm sure she's awake by now. Want me to go get her?"

"Sure. She'll probably be more open to you right now than to me. Don't you think?"

"Uh-huh." She patted his damp head. "I love you, Johnny."

As he refilled his glass with water, he knew he was lucky. No, he was blessed. With both Michelle and Grace. He probably didn't deserve either one of them, but God had been generous. Now hopefully he could convince Grace to forgive him . . . again.

"*Johnny!*" Grace's voice sliced through the house with an urgency that cut him to the core as he sprinted from the kitchen and up the stairs.

*"What? What is it?"* he yelled as he raced to Grace's room, bracing himself for whatever had happened and praying that it was not the worst thing imaginable.

"It's Grace!" Michelle held out a note to him. "She's left."

For a moment he felt a small surge of relief—at least she wasn't hurt, or worse. Running away wasn't the same as being dead. But as he read the note, he wasn't so sure. Grace had set out to launch her music career. She hadn't included many of the details about how she planned to do this impossible feat. Although it seemed apparent that somehow she'd gotten it into her head that Sapphire was interested in her. Was she crazy? Johnny knew enough about the music business to know that this was a bad path to take. An innocent young girl out there trying to make her break and get a few gigs and earn enough to keep from starving—well, it wasn't a pretty picture. He'd seen it enough times to know. Not only were the odds against her for succeeding in the music business, but they were stacked up against her a bunch of other horrible ways as well. Really, this was a father's worst nightmare. Or very nearly.

"What do we do?" Michelle asked with teary eyes.

"Pray?"

"Yes, of course. We need to ask God's guidance and direction on this," she nodded. "Do you think she really could've made it all the way to Los Angeles?"

He thought hard. "I don't know. But that's where Sapphire is located."

She nodded. "Even if she was headed there, how do you think she got there?"

"Train? Bus?" He frowned. "Did she have much money?"

"Not that I know of." Michelle was going through Grace's things now, acting like a detective who was trying to find a clue to the mystery.

"We can try her cell," Johnny said. "But she probably won't answer."

Michelle nodded and then let out a choked sob. "What do we do?"

Johnny pulled her into his arms. "I'm so sorry, babe. I shouldn't have gotten angry at her like I did. But we'll figure it out. I promise you. I'll find her."

"According to the date on the note, she took off last night. Where could she have slept?" Michelle asked between sobs. "Where is she now?"

Grace was relieved that she'd been able to sleep on the red-eye flight to Los Angeles. But she'd been so exhausted after her hair-raising getaway last night that it wasn't really surprising she'd conked out on her second flight. She didn't even want to think about how she'd taken a ride from complete strangers— a couple of college-aged guys that she'd found at the diner in town. Noticing her guitar, they'd started chatting with her about music. As it turned out, they just happened to be on their way to Birmingham too.

They seemed respectable enough, but after having been taught for years not to talk to—let alone ride with—strangers, she knew she could've been making a big mistake. Thankfully, she was not. The guys turned out to be great, and they even dropped her off at the airport, telling her not to forget them when she became a big star.

Her flight out of Birmingham was a short little hop on a small jet that seemed to bounce over the turbulence all the way to Atlanta. And when she arrived, she had a long lay-over until her next flight. However, she couldn't complain because she had told Mossy's assistant she wanted to leave on Sunday night, and she had refused to back down. Fortunately, the assistant had made arrangements for Grace to spend the night in an airport hotel. So with her guitar case and bag, she boarded a hotel shuttle bus at about ten o'clock that night. But because her morning flight was an early one and she worried she might oversleep, and because she was feeling uneasy about her parents, and mostly because she was so excited about this adventure she was embarking on, she had spent most of the night wide awake.

It was no wonder she'd slept soundly on the flight to LA. But now that she was here and it was morning and no airport security or police had tried to stop her—which she'd been expecting the whole time—she felt free as a bird. As she rode down the escalator to baggage claim, she suppressed the urge to spread her wings and pretend to fly. After all, she wasn't a child anymore.

She didn't have any bags to claim, but Mossy's assistant had said that was where passengers were picked up. And sure enough, as soon as she stepped off the escalator, there was a lineup of drivers, all holding up signs with people's names on them. And to her delight there was a man dressed in a crisp black suit and holding up a sign that said *Grace Trey*. It if had been written in lights, she wouldn't have been one bit happier.

"I'm Grace Trey," she told him.

"Welcome to LA, Miss Trey." He reached for her bag and guitar.

"Thank you!" She beamed at him.

"Right this way."

He led her out to where a sleek black limo was parked near the taxis. She tried not to feel too smug as she walked past grown-ups waiting in line for taxis. And she could feel them looking at her, probably wondering who she was, as her driver opened the door for her. Holding her head high, she slipped into the limo. She felt like a million bucks.

As the limo pulled out of the airport, Grace looked out the windows. It seemed that palm trees were growing everywhere. A nice touch though. She stared in awe as they traveled through what seemed familiar scenes—probably things she'd seen in movies—until eventually she knew they were in Hollywood.

She wanted to pinch herself. Was this really happening? Or was it just another one of her wild and crazy daydreams?

"Here we are, Miss," he said as he pulled up to the curb. "Sapphire Music."

Suddenly she wished she'd taken some time to check her hair and makeup. She wasn't ready for this. Fumbling in her bag, she pulled out a small compact and did a quick inventory. Thankfully, and despite a long night, she didn't look too worse for wear. But, really, she should have planned this entrance a little better. She wasn't even sure who she was meeting with this morning. Although Mossy's assistant had promised that Mossy would be there.

"There you go," the driver said as he set her bag on the sidewalk next to her. "Good luck." He handed her the guitar case.

"Thanks." She giggled as she looped a strap over her shoulder. She looked up at the tall building and took in a deep breath. This was it. Really it. The Sapphire Music building. This was for real. Now what?

She went through the glass doors into what appeared to be a security check. Not unlike the airport this morning. Once she got through there, she entered a big modern-looking lobby. All glass and chrome and leather. But what really captured her attention were the big flat screens on the all the walls. They were playing various music videos and sound, and the feeling in this space was knock-your-socks-off incredible. She could've just sat there all day, soaking it in.

However, she reminded herself that was not why she was here. Now she spotted a large sleek desk with an attractive brunette standing behind it. Holding her head high and trying not to look too burdened down by her bags, she went up and told the woman her name. "I'm here to see Frank Mostin."

"Oh, yes." She nodded. "Mr. Mostin asked me to give him a call when you arrived." She pointed to one of the long leather couches. "Please, have a seat. I'm sure he'll be down soon."

As Grace walked over to the sitting area, she noticed what looked like a big celebrity walking past with a man in a gray suit. Not that she knew who it was exactly, but just the same she did a double take. Then, not wanting to look like a starstruck hick, she sat down on the couch and tried not to gape. Instead she just gazed around in wonder. Everywhere she looked there was something fascinating to see. Besides the videos playing on the flat screens, there were framed gold and platinum records and promotional posters of singers she admired, including Renae Taylor. It was like a musician's paradise. And the palm trees outside just seemed to prove it.

She didn't mind waiting for Mossy and was slightly caught off guard to see him approaching her, not wearing a suit like when she'd first met him, but dressed casually in jeans and a suede jacket. "There she is!" he exclaimed happily. "Good to see you again."

She stood and smiled. But suddenly she felt awkward as he shook her hand. All this was so out of her element. "Thanks," she mumbled. "You too."

"Your flight okay?"

"Yeah, yeah. It was great. Thanks for the limo too." She was trying to act like a grown-up, but she felt more like a grade-school kid. Way out of her comfort zone. *Come on*, she told herself, *just chill*.

"You hungry?"

She shrugged. "I'm fine."

He laughed. "Well, I'm starving. Come on."

She felt slightly disappointed as they exited the building. But she told herself they would be coming back. Besides, she really was hungry. Or she thought she should be. However, she wasn't even sure if she'd be able to eat. This was all so exciting. So much more than she'd expected.

Mossy chatted away at her as he drove her through the city. "We're going to the Palm Restaurant," he said. "West Hollywood." He told her a bit about some of the places she was seeing as they rode, pointing out sights and giving her bits of Hollywood history. She could tell he was trying to help her relax. And she appreciated it.

After they were seated in the swanky restaurant, Mossy looked her straight in the eyes. "I'll be honest with you, Grace, I don't like doing this behind Johnny's back. But I get it."

She nodded. "Yeah. It's not easy for me either."

"Some parents just don't appreciate that their kids grow up and have dreams of their own."

"That's my dad." She sighed as she laid the napkin on her lap and picked up the menu. "If you Googled the word *over-protective*, you'd probably find a photo of my dad posted there."

Mossy laughed. "Well, when you're on iTunes and Pandora, I'm guessing he'll come around."

As the waitress filled their coffee cups, she smiled to imagine how cool it was going to be. Staking her claim to fame—it felt awesome.

"Okay, now . . ." Mossy studied her closely. "Let me ask you something, Grace."

"Yeah." She laid the menu back down.

"You've come a couple thousand miles. You left everything you know. You don't have any family out here, right?"

"No."

*"What do you want?"*

Grace considered this—what a big question to be asked first thing in the morning. Still, she already knew her answer. "I want to blow people away with my music," she declared. "And I know I have what it takes."

Mossy barely nodded, but she sensed his silent approval. Just then the waitress returned and, after fumbling through the menu, Grace finally made a choice, and the waitress left again.

"So you want to blow people away." Mossy made a crooked grin, and she wondered if he was mocking her. "You and a million other girls."

"Yeah, well," she felt like someone was about to jerk the rug out from beneath her. Was Mossy going to knock her down to reality too? Was he just like her father?

"But there's one thing you have that those million other girls don't," he continued.

She sighed. "Yeah, I know. A dad with a famous song. I get it."

"No." He shook his head. "You have me."

"Oh?"

"Don't get me wrong, Grace. Being your dad's daughter, that's a good angle. And just like I did with him, I can do with you. I can take you anywhere you want to go. If you're willing to put in the work and do what I tell you, I will get you there."

Grace felt hopeful again. But then her cell phone rang, distracting her. Seeing it was "home" calling, she hit decline and dropped it back into her bag, smiling at Mossy. "I'm a hard worker," she assured him. "I'm willing to do what it takes to be a star. I don't expect anyone to just hand it to me. I want to earn it myself."

"That's what I like to hear. But I've been in the biz long enough to know that no one gets there alone. You need help along the way." He grinned. "That's why I'm here."

As Mossy continued to talk about the business and what needed to be done, Grace tried not to imagine what her parents were doing or thinking. Sure, Mom would be freaking. She'd probably be pacing and calling all of Grace's friends. For all Grace knew, Mom might've called the FBI or National Guard by now. But, really, what could anyone do? And Dad, well, he'd probably be glad to have her out of his hair. He'd have no one to mess up his perfect little worship services from now on. He was probably throwing a celebration party by now.

"I've already begun booking you gigs," he explained. "And invites will go out to every A & R exec in town—including my friends at Sapphire—"

"Wait," she stopped him. "Why not just sign with Sapphire. You work there, don't you?"

"I'm a *manager*, Grace. I don't work for any one label. Sure I work in the Sapphire building. They're a few floors up. But I rep musicians."

"Oh, well, on the phone you made it sound like—"

"I know, I know. It's hard to explain, but you'll figure it all out in time. This is how business is done in this town." He sipped his coffee. "So tell me about yourself and your music, Grace."

Grace was still stuck on the fact that Mossy did not work for Sapphire. Hadn't he told her he did? Or was she just that naïve and inexperienced that she'd misunderstood. Whatever the case, she would have to sort it out later. "Well, I grew up loving music. I've been playing piano and guitar practically since I can remember."

"You said you've written songs?" he questioned.

She just nodded, uncertain of how to answer. And she almost wished she hadn't lied about that. But when he'd offered her this big opportunity, how could she possibly admit that she was a flop as a songwriter? Besides that was then; this was now. Surely she could pop out a song with so much at stake, especially if she really put her whole self into it.

"They're not religious, right?" he pressed.

"No. Like I said, I write, and, I mean, I think my songs are really good, but . . . the more I think about it, I'm not totally sure they're ready to record yet."

"That's all right. You'll have time to work on them. I'll push for an album, but I doubt we'll get it right away."

She tried to relax again, but that bit about songwriting had left her feeling nervous. What if Mossy knew what a fraud she was? Would he send her packing?

"So, who's your favorite singer?" he asked as the waitress set the bill on the table.

"Probably Renae Taylor."

He made a thoughtful nod. "Yeah. I see some Renae in you. We play it right, maybe you'll open for her."

"No way." Grace felt a mixture of angst and hope.

His dark eyes twinkled. "Why not? Then one day maybe she'll open for you."

She tried not to look as thrilled as she felt to hear this. Did he really believe that? Or was he just stringing her along?

"You keep working on your songs," he said. "But step one is just a daughter singing her dad's hit, anywhere and everywhere. That I can sell. Any questions?"

She shook her head no, but the part about working on her songs threw her. What songs? What if she couldn't get a song out? Still she was determined not to worry about that yet. For now she just wanted to enjoy this ride, her ride to stardom.

# Chapter 8

Mossy's assistant had promised Grace that she'd have a place to live in LA. But when Mossy drove her into a less than glamorous neighborhood, Grace tried not to show her disappointment. Like he'd said, and she'd agreed, she needed to work her way into this business. No one was handing her anything. Besides that, she was finally going to be on her own—no parents breathing down her neck, studying her every move, criticizing her music. This was her ticket to freedom!

"So, uh, this is it," Mossy said as he stopped in front of a door on the third floor and handed her the key. "You think you'll be okay?"

"Sure." She turned the key and opened the door, walking into a small furnished apartment. "This is mine?"

"Yeah, just for now." Mossy sounded uncertain.

"For *now?*"

"It's all about delivering, Grace. Things go well, you'll buy a house in Malibu."

She smiled as she looked around. Sure, it wasn't the fabulous apartment she'd imagined, but it was hers. The little kitchen and living room were hers. The bedroom, which was smaller than her bedroom at home, was hers. She peeked out the window and was surprised to see a church across the street. Her eyes locked onto the cross for a moment, and then she pulled the drapes closed. Turning back to Mossy, she could see that he was uneasy about something.

"So, what do you think?" he asked in a worried tone.

"I love it," she proclaimed. "Thank you."

Now he looked relieved. "Okay, kid. I'll leave you to it. My assistant put some food in the kitchen. And a few things she thought you might need since you left Alabama in such a hurry. Anyway, I'm sure you need a chance to catch your breath. But keep your phone on. I'll be in touch."

She thanked him again, and before he left, he reminded her to lock the door. He winked. "You're not in Alabama anymore."

She did lock the door, and then she proceeded to examine everything in the apartment more closely, opening cupboards and closets. Just like Mossy had said, there was food in the kitchen. And the bathroom even had some essentials like soap and shampoo and toothpaste. The assistant had even thought to put hangers in the closet. She went from room to room, checking it all out. She couldn't believe it—her own place. She took her time unpacking. And then she sat down to play guitar, hoping that being in this new place—with no one trying to control her—she would be able to write a song. She played and made notes and played some more. But the song, if there was a song, seemed to be stuck somewhere inside of her.

"Doesn't matter," she told herself as she put her guitar away. "This is only my first day here. I have plenty of time." And feeling celebratory, she pulled out her iPod and popped in her earbuds and, listening to a high-energy Renae Taylor song, she happily danced all around her apartment. If Renae couldn't inspire her music, who could? Finally she was tired and decided to take a nap. After all, she'd only had about four hours sleep on the flight from Atlanta. But after about an hour of fidgeting on the couch, which was not as comfy as it looked, she felt too antsy to sleep.

She sat up and looked at her watch. If it was two o'clock here, it was four in Alabama. Rachel would just be getting off work in the bookstore. Grace waited a few minutes, giving Rachel time to clock out and go outside to her car, and then she called.

"Grace!" Rachel exclaimed. "Where are you?"

"LA," Grace said calmly.

"What?"

"I'm in Los Angeles. I've already been to Sapphire Music, had breakfast in Hollywood and now—"

"But why? *Why* are you doing this? Don't you realize your parents are frantic? They called me this morning, thinking that I knew all about it and—"

"Sorry, Rach. I suspected they'd call you."

"Why didn't you tell me what you were doing?" she demanded.

"I purposely left you out of the loop because I knew you'd be the first one they called."

"But I'm your best friend . . . at least I thought I was."

"You are my best friend," Grace insisted. "You are the first one I've called." Now she told Rachel all about her cool new apartment. And, as she walked from room to room, she knew that she was painting a lot better picture than it really was, but why not? Like Mossy had said, this was just the beginning.

"And Mossy thinks I'm better than my dad," she continued as she stopped in the bedroom. "He's told me that, like, ten times."

"Uh-huh, so how long you think you'll be there?"

"I don't know." Grace flopped back onto the bed. "Hopefully forever. I mean, not forever, but I guess however long it takes."

"Okay," Rachel sounded unusually subdued.

"What?" Grace demanded. "What's wrong?"

"Nothing. I'm just . . . well, you didn't even say good-bye."

"I already told you I'm sorry, Rach. But, seriously, if my dad had known, he would've killed me. I had to do it like this." She sat up and looked around the small dismal room. "I know this is where I'm supposed to be. It's incredible. Mossy already has shows planned and everything."

"That . . . uh, that's neat."

"Neat?" Grace stood up and went to the window. Was that the best Rachel could do? She opened the drapes and looked out at the church again, staring blankly at the cross.

"What do you want me to say, Grace?" Rachel let out a long sigh. "You've always been amazing, but . . . I just . . . I didn't expect it to happen like this."

"Like *what?*"

"Like this! I mean are you even gonna call your parents?"

Grace couldn't believe it—why was Rachel acting like this? Was she eighteen or eight? "Are you crazy? I call my parents, and Dad gives me the biggest lecture of my life. Why do you think I wanted outta there? Dad has to see that I can make it on my own."

"And that will make everything okay, right?" Rachel's tone dripped with skepticism.

"Look," Grace said slowly. "I left a note. All right? They know where I am."

"Not really. I mean your mom sounded really upset. Just let them hear your voice. Let them know you're okay."

"If it's so important to you, why don't you let them know?"

"I'm not their daughter, Grace. You are."

"You know, Rach, I thought that you of all people would understand. I mean, I even had this crazy idea that you'd actually be happy for me."

"I am, I guess."

"You *guess?*"

"You know what I mean."

"Yeah. I think I do. You know what else I think?" Grace's grip tightened on her phone. "I think you should move in with my parents and be the perfect daughter they always wanted."

There was a long, silent pause now. Grace wondered if Rachel had hung up.

"Why are you acting like this?" Rachel finally asked in a hurt tone.

Grace felt guilty now. Why did she want to hurt Rachel like that? "Look, tell them I'm all right if you want to, *okay*? I gotta go."

As he ripped the suitcase down from the top of the closet, Johnny knew what he had to do. He tossed the case onto the bed, zipped it open, and began throwing clothes in.

"What are you doing?" Michelle demanded when she walked into the hurricane of clothes that were flying around, some landing in the suitcase, most missing it.

"What does it look like I'm doing?" He tossed a pair of jeans toward the case.

She picked up a T-shirt and proceeded to fold it neatly. Clearing the messy pile on the suitcase, she laid it flat and started to fold another. "You honestly think she'll listen to you, Johnny?"

"I'm not going there to talk." He tossed some socks onto the bed.

"What? Are you going to drag her back home? Kicking and screaming on the flight?"

"Maybe," he growled as he tossed several pairs of boxers her direction.

"Johnny, think about what you're doing!"

He came over and started shoving his clothes into the suitcase, trying to make it all fit, which was just not happening. "I don't get you!" He stood up straight and shook his fist in the air. "You *like* what she's done? You approve?"

"Of course not! But she's eighteen! And maybe if you hadn't been so hard on her, maybe none of this would've happened!"

Johnny just glared at her now. How could she say that? Taking Grace's side in this? Blaming him for Grace's rebellion? Did she blame him for Mossy's betrayal as well? Luring her out there? Like all this was his fault? He picked up the mess of a suitcase and heaved it across the room where it hit the wall with a dull thud, then slid onto the ground in a heap of clothes. And now, it figured, Michelle was crying. Well, fine, let her cry. Maybe she would feel better when she was done. In the meantime he had other things to do.

He went down to his study and picked up his phone. He'd already called Mossy a dozen times and left as many angry messages. This time he planned to threaten Mossy with a lawsuit. Even if he didn't have a legal leg to stand on, he might be able to put the fear of God into him. But to his surprise Mossy answered.

"It's about time you picked up," Johnny snapped at him. "I've just about had it with you and—"

"Hey, Johnny," Moss said smooth as silk. "What's up, man?"

Johnny took a deep breath. If he wanted Mossy's cooperation, he would have to handle this differently. "I think you know what's up," Johnny said carefully.

"Sorry I've missed your calls," Mossy told him. "It's been busy here."

"Look, Moss, this is wrong, and you know it."

"What, Johnny?" Mossy sounded offended now. "What's wrong?"

"My only kid. You rip her right out from under my nose."

"Rip her from under your nose? Are you serious?"

Johnny was pacing now, back and forth like a caged tiger ready to go for blood. "I'm dead serious, Moss. You stole my baby, and I want her back. I'm coming after you, man."

"Are you insane?" Mossy sounded indignant now. "I'm taking a chance on her. I came for you, remember? But you kicked me to the curb again. Just like you used to do."

"Wait a minute!" He stopped pacing. "I honored every agreement we ever had. This had *nothing* to with that, and you know it!"

"Hey, I poured my life into you, man. Even when you fell apart, I stuck by you."

"And I gave you my publishing!" Johnny was pacing again.

"I never asked for it. All I know is, after twenty years I come to you for one favor. And you. Said. No."

Johnny wanted to hit something . . . or someone. "How can you do this to me, man?"

"Do what?"

"Steal my little girl."

"Listen, Johnny, I'm not going to tell you this again. I did not steal anyone's *little girl*. Your *adult* daughter, who happens to be brilliant, came to *me*. What did you expect me to do? Turn her away? Ignore her talent?"

"What do you mean she came to you? I don't believe it. You cast out a line and pulled her in. I know you."

"You don't know—"

"You promised you'd make her a star, didn't you? You told her she'd be living the big life and—"

"For your information, Johnny, your daughter came to me. When she saw you turn me down that day, her musician's mind went to work. She made a demo of 'Misunderstood,' and she sent it to me. Naturally, she didn't want you to know about any of this because, as you've just shown me today, you would've flipped out. Seems that Grace knows you a lot better than I do."

Johnny sat down in his desk chair, trying to process this. Grace had approached Mossy, not the other way around.

"And just so you know, Johnny, Grace's demo was brilliant. Everyone who's seen it is totally taken with her. She's got real star quality. So, really, it's pretty simple. When plan A didn't fly, I moved on to plan B. To be perfectly honest, I'm already liking it a lot better anyway."

"Don't do this, Mossy." Johnny leaned forward on his desk, running his hands through his hair. Somehow he had to stop this machine, but he had no idea how. "She's just a kid," he said meekly.

"You know, your daughter has you pegged, man, she really does! I get this isn't *your thing* anymore, but now you wanna kill her dream too? Listen, I got a new talent that starts gigging tomorrow, and I gotta lot of work to do before then." He paused as if to let this sink into Johnny's already throbbing head. "Give my love to Shelly." Then the phone line went dead. Mossy had hung up on him.

Now Johnny did something that he hadn't done in years. He cupped his head in his hands and he cried. Just like a broken little kid, he cried and cried. And then he did what he should've done right from the start, he humbled himself and asked for God's help to untangle this mess.

# Chapter 9

Grace knew this was her big night, her first gig in a real club. A Hollywood club. Her emotions were a gnarled ball of threads—excitement, fear, hopefulness, anxiety—all of it was twisted inside of her. "Just breathe," Mossy said as he handed the keys to the parking lot valet. "You're going to be fine."

She looked down at the outfit she had sweated bullets over and hoped she got it right. First she'd wanted to dress older and had several outfits lined up that would've helped her pass for mid-twenties. But then she remembered how Mossy had told her just to wear whatever she was comfortable in. So she'd done that. And now she wasn't sure she had made the right decision. In jeans and a flowing white blouse and vest, she didn't exactly look like she was on her way to Sunday school, but she didn't look like she was about to perform in an LA club either.

Grace could hear the bass thumping outside the club. She watched as several scantily dressed twenty-something women went inside, followed by a couple of guys in that same age range. Grace knew she didn't fit in with this crowd . . . didn't belong here. But she also knew this was how singers got started. Mossy had already told her that even her dad had paid his dues singing at clubs like this. Everyone did.

She braced herself as they went into the dimly lit club. Naturally the music was louder in here, and, to her disappointment, the band playing seemed substandard. Although that could work to her benefit too—if she was better than they were. However, she was unsure of why people were here. Wasn't it primarily to dance? Did anyone really care whether the music was good or not?

"Get a feel for the room," Mossy said loudly, to be heard over the music. "I'll tell Tommy we're here."

Grace nodded, watching as Mossy went off in search of the club manager. She tried to act nonchalant as she watched the patrons interacting with one another. But the more she watched, the more it became crystal clear. People were here for two things—to drink and to hook up. Music was secondary. In fact, it probably would make no difference if a DJ was working this joint. She glanced across the room to see that Mossy was talking to a man that she figured was Tommy. The two seemed caught up in their own little world, and Mossy was completely oblivious that she was over here, practically having a panic attack as she cowered in the corner. Everything inside of her told her to run—run fast and don't look back.

She glanced over her shoulder to see a man who appeared to be in his forties staring at her with way too much interest. Oh, great, had she managed to attract a stalker? Or perhaps it was an undercover cop who had figured out that she was underage. She felt her eyes growing wide as he came directly toward her. Running seemed ridiculous since she would probably be safer in here anyway.

"You must be Grace," he said loudly.

She blinked. Was she imagining this?

"You're Grace Trey, right?" He smiled and she relaxed a little.

"Yes."

He reached to shake her hand. "Larry Reynolds, Sapphire Music."

Grace tried to act perfectly natural—as if she wasn't blown away that the president of one of the biggest music labels knew her name. "Pleased to meet you," she said in a surprisingly natural-sounding voice.

"Big fan of you dad," he told her. "Loved your demo."

A smile of relief crept onto her face and, as she thanked him, she looked at him more closely. For a man his age, he was attractive and nicely dressed.

"I'm looking forward to hearing you perform tonight," he said warmly.

"Thanks." She made a stiff smile. "I'm feeling a little nervous."

He nodded. "Perfectly natural."

Then, just like that, Mossy was gathering her up, giving his regard to Larry, and swooping her away. It wasn't until they were backstage that she spoke her mind. "You didn't tell me Larry Reynolds would be at my first show!" she exclaimed.

"You never know! They show up when they show up."

"They don't call first or anything?"

"Look, just forget he's even here. This night is about you."

She pressed her lips together, trying to breathe evenly, trying to relax.

"Listen to me," Mossy said calmly and slowly, "you've heard this song your whole life. You and the band rehearsed for over an hour. And it felt good, right?"

She nodded. "Yeah. I guess."

"It was great," he assured her. "Things move fast around here. Just relax, Grace. This is *your* time. Enjoy it." He handed her a bottle of water. "Just breathe and focus and relax. You're gonna rock this place." He winked at her. "I'll be down in the cheap seats. Remember, you know what you're doing. You know this song. Just own it, babe."

And just like that he was gone. She tried to replay everything he'd just said. She tried to breathe and relax, taking little sips of cool water. She considered praying, like she might've done before . . . before she'd taken her life into her own hands. Now she didn't think praying would help. *I can do this*, she told herself. *I know I can.*

Now she could hear someone talking into the mic, and she peeked out to see Tommy out in front. "Well, I'm sure you all remember Johnny Trey." He laughed like this was funny. "Anyway, some of you old-timers do. And the rest of you have probably heard that Swedish kid singing Johnny's song 'Misunderstood' enough times. But we got something really special for you tonight. We have Johnny Trey's daughter right here. Yep, friends, she's making her debut tonight. Singing the Johnny Trey classic, 'Misunderstood.' Put your hands together for *Grace Trey.*"

The crowd reacted appropriately, clapping and cheering, as Grace made her way to center stage, taking a moment to adjust the mic. She made a feeble smile as she gazed out over the crowd, spotting Mossy and Larry near the front. Now she glanced back at the band to make sure they were set. But as she turned back around, her guitar neck whacked the mic stand, and the sound was all squeaky, and some of the people laughed. Collecting herself, she adjusted the mic, forcing another smile.

"Sorry," she told them. Steadying herself, she took in another deep breath then, ready to go for it, she gave a nod to the band and counted it off. "One, two, three, four—" And then she just leaped into it. She could hear the tremor in her voice at first, but it smoothed out by the second line. And by the time she hit the chorus, she was in the groove. By the second verse she knew she was rocking the house. They loved her and weren't afraid to show it. Even better, she was loving this!

But before the song was finished, she noticed Larry getting ready to leave. She watched, worried that she'd failed, but then she saw him giving Mossy a nod, and she hoped that meant something. Still, she wished he would've stayed to the end. She wished he would've heard the crowd exploding into applause. They liked her!

Backstage, she hurried to find Mossy. "What happened to Larry Reynolds?" she demanded breathlessly.

"Don't you worry about that."

"But he left early," she said as she unstrapped her guitar.

"He left because he'd seen enough." Mossy grinned. "Don't you get it? He liked you, Grace."

"Are you serious?"

"Don't get too excited. We don't have a deal yet. But, my dear, you just blew away Sapphire Music."

She controlled herself from dancing. "Oh, my goodness!" She covered her mouth with her hand. "I was so nervous."

"Well, you delivered."

"This is incredible! I don't even want to leave now."

"Then don't. Stay and enjoy it. I'm gonna grab a statement from Tommy for marketing. Go have fun. Meet your fans." He started to go, then stopped. "Hey." He looked her in the eyes. "You did great, Grace. I'm really proud of you. I mean that."

She felt touched by this kindness from him. She tried not to compare it to all the criticism she was used to getting when it came to her music. No, she was not going to let anything spoil this moment. She went out into the club again, and although she felt slightly more comfortable than before, she was still clearly a misfit here. Not only were these people all older; they still seemed to have only a couple of things on their minds. Things she had no interest in. Even so, a few of them greeted her, giving her an occasional high five or "congrats." But mostly she was just another girl.

Feeling a bit disenchanted, she decided to go over to where her band was seated on the other side of the room. At least she could make some small talk with them. But about halfway there, a couple of guys seemed intent on intercepting her.

"Hey," a well-built guy said in a friendly voice.

"Hi," she said a bit crisply.

"Let me buy you a drink," he offered in a slightly slurred voice.

She wanted to point out that he didn't need any more alcohol but instead told him, "No, thanks."

But instead of accepting this, he got even closer to her, leaning in close enough that she could smell the booze on his breath. "No, I'm serious," he said. "Jus' one drink."

Feeling nervous, she pointed to her band. "No, that's okay. Actually I have to . . . um . . . they're waiting for me over there."

Feeling like she barely escaped her drunken friend, she slunk over to the where her band was sitting around a table and, like everyone else, drinking heavily.

"You were hot," the bass player told her. "You need a band, we're in."

"Right on." Grace smiled. "You guys are great."

Still feeling jazzed from her successful performance, she visited happily with the band for awhile. And then, for some reason she looked up, glancing over to the entrance where a way-too-familiar man was standing—staring at her. Dad! What was he doing here? She studied his face carefully, expecting him to be enraged at finding her in such a place, but all she could see in his eyes was sadness. However, she knew he could be tricky like that. One moment she thought he cared, and the next moment he was smacking her ego to the ground. For nearly a minute they just stared across the room at each other, and finally she knew she had to face him.

"Excuse me," she told the band. "Something I need to attend to." Then she walked across the crowded room with a newfound confidence. She wondered if her dad had seen her performance. If he had seen the crowd's reaction.

"Let's go outside," she told him loudly to be heard over the music.

He nodded, opening the door for her.

"What are you doing here?" she asked when they were on the sidewalk.

"I'm here because I love you," he said quietly.

"Did you see me up there?" she asked hopefully.

He nodded, but she could tell by his expression that he had not approved.

She was crushed. "Yeah. And I'm sure you hated how I played your song."

"Grace, I know I haven't always been the best father. But baby, think about what you're doing. Running away. All the deception." He lowered his voice. "Do you honestly believe you're doing this for God? Or does that even matter to you anymore?"

Why was he doing this? Why did he keep trying to hold her back? Forcing her into his mold of what a good daughter should be? Why couldn't he just accept her as she was? Was she really that bad? That unlovable?

"Listen, if you want to go solo, you want to play my song, that's fine. I don't care about that right now. But let's talk about it, okay? Don't do it behind our backs . . . you're not ready for this."

Now she wasn't just hurt; she was angry. Could he really be this clueless? Did he not see how the crowd loved her? Of course, she was ready. She was more than ready. "Weren't you even watching?"

"I'm not talking about the music, Grace. Come home. Mom and I both—"

"Johnny." Mossy joined them with a surprised expression.

Feeling like her protector had just shown up, Grace moved closer to Mossy, standing defiantly next to him.

"If I'd known you were here, I would've had them introduce you, Johnny."

Johnny glared at Mossy like he wanted to punch him. But his expression softened when he looked at Grace. She knew what he was thinking . . . he'd come to take his little girl home. He wanted his puppet back, wanted to pull her strings. She was not having any of it.

"Really, Dad?" She narrowed her eyes, trying to disguise her tears with anger. "Did you honestly come all this way just to tell me I'm wrong again? That I'm not good enough? That I'm not ready for this? What a waste of airfare."

"No," he said quickly. "Let's go somewhere. Let's talk."

She felt angry tears streaking down her cheeks but hoped they weren't visible in this dim light. "No," she told him in a strong voice. "This is what I want. And I don't care what you think." Now she couldn't stop herself from wiping the tears. "Tell Mom I love her." She turned away from him wanting to go back into the club, except that now she was crying. So instead of going inside, she paused near the door trying to get her emotions under control. As she stood there, she listened, curious as to whether Mossy would have additional words for her dad. She hoped he did. After all, wasn't a manager supposed to help protect his clients?

"Kids," Mossy said in an indifferent sort of way.

"Listen," her dad said with startling intensity. "You hurt my daughter, I'll find you."

"And you call yourself a man of faith?" Mossy's tone was slightly degrading now. "Look, Johnny, I'm not gonna hurt her. I'm gonna help her get what she wants. Something you obviously can't or won't do." She heard the shuffle of footsteps. "Have a safe flight home," Mossy called as he came over to the entrance, jumping slightly when he saw her lurking in the shadows.

She held her forefinger over her lips to shush him from saying anything. She did not want Dad to come over and make one last attempt to get her to go home with him. She knew how persistent he could be, how he could make a scene if he wanted. But hearing his footsteps leading away, she knew he'd given up. At least for the night. If he would only back off for long enough, perhaps she'd have the chance to show him that he was wrong—that she *was* ready for this.

# Chapter 10

The next few days passed in a happy blur for Grace. Signing a contract with Sapphire Music. Being featured in a small article in *Billboard Magazine*. Becoming the new talk of the town. It was all happening so quickly. Her dreams were coming true. And tonight, dressed to the nines, Grace was attending a fancy cocktail part at Larry Reynolds's luxurious home in the Hollywood Hills. To say she was sitting on top of the world was an understatement. She was flying high above it.

She and Mossy entered the massive foyer, and Grace was immediately aware of the sounds of guests and music and the tinkling of glasses. She'd never felt like such a grown-up before. If only Rachel could see her now. Or not. Because she felt pretty sure that Rachel, like her dad, would not approve. For that reason she pushed all thoughts of Alabama and Homewood to the darkest recesses of her mind. Tonight was a night for celebration. This was her night!

Larry Reynolds spotted them from across the room. Coming over, he warmly welcomed them, taking both of Grace's hands in his. "Look at you. The woman of the hour. How does it feel?"

She giggled. "Pretty cool."

He exchanged an amused glance with Mossy. "Pretty cool? We just signed her first big contract, and it's pretty cool?"

Grace laughed. "Sorry. It's fabulous. I'm totally jazzed. Okay?"

He nodded. "That's better."

"And you saw the article in *Billboard* today," Mossy said to Larry.

"Oh, yeah." Larry waved over to where a waiter was passing by with a tray of sparkling drinks. Probably champagne. "I really liked that they used photos of Grace and her dad."

She frowned. "Me and Dad?"

"You didn't see it?"

"I didn't get it to her yet," Mossy explained. "Yeah, Grace, we gave them an old photo of your dad, he was just a little older than you. And one of your publicity photos that you just had taken a few days ago. It was a real nice layout."

"Sure was." Larry reached for a glass of champagne, holding it out to Grace. "Can we drink to you?"

She made a nervous grimace that probably told everyone in the room that she'd never touched alcohol before.

Larry nodded. "Oh, I get it. No problem."

Mossy reached for a glass too. Then the waiter, who obviously didn't get it, held the tray out for Grace, waiting for her to take a glass.

"Oh, why not." She giggled as she reached for one.

"Here's to you," Larry said as he held up his glass. "To a bright future for a bright star. I'm proud to have you on the Sapphire team, Grace."

They clinked glasses, and Grace had her first taste of champagne. She tried not to wrinkle her nose, but her first reaction was that of wonder. She wondered how anyone could stand this stuff. Even so, she pretended to enjoy it as the conversation continued.

"The way you play reminds me of your dad," Larry told her.

"Thanks," she said with a bit of uncertainty. "He taught me to play."

"I have a lot of respect for your dad," Larry said. "He has conviction."

She made an awkward smile, then looked around the beautiful room. "Your home is amazing," she said.

"Thank you."

"I'll bet the view is fabulous."

He nodded. "You'll have to check it out later."

Now Mossy and Larry launched into business talk and, if it hadn't been directly related to her, she would've left from boredom. But because she was the subject, she hung on, trying to act like she was taking it all in. At the same time she was trying to take in the other celebrities she was spotting around the room. It was like the who's who of Sapphire was here tonight. Any minute, Renae Taylor might walk in.

"Do you have a time frame on an album?" Mossy was saying to Larry.

"No. Let's record the single, then the video. See how they trend."

"Sure." Mossy nodded.

"And even if 'Misunderstood' does hit, how much is Grace, how much is the father-daughter remake story, you know?"

"She's the real deal, Larry."

Larry nodded, sipping his champagne and running his eyes around the busy room as if he was hunting for someone. "Of course."

"What about a follow-up single? An original."

"We've talked about it."

"Be a great step before an album, don't you think?"

Larry nodded again, but Grace could see his eyes were on something else. Make that someone else. She followed his gaze to see that the gorgeously stylish Kendra Burroughs had arrived. The fashion diva was slowly making her way toward them as if she had a purpose in mind. Grace knew who she was—stylist to the stars—but she hadn't met her.

Larry gave Kendra a wave but continued talking business to Mossy. "Well, if the single does get traction, we'll do a radio tour. We'll definitely want a follow-up in place by then."

"Absolutely," Mossy said eagerly.

Larry turned his attention to Grace. "Tell you what. Why don't you demo an original for us?"

Grace tried not to flinch. "Sure. No problem." Mossy shot her a wink.

"Again, no promises," Larry reminded. "Let's stay clear on this—it's all about the numbers."

"Of course," Mossy agreed.

Now Kendra was joining them. "Frank Mostin," she said. "Haven't seen you in a while."

"How are you, Kendra?"

"Excellent."

"Grace, this is Kendra Burroughs," Larry said. "Artist development. She'll be your image maker."

Grace felt a surge of delight. Kendra Burroughs was going to style her! Did it get any better than this? "Hi," Grace said shyly.

"Your pictures do not do you justice, girl. You are stunning."

"Thank you." Grace tried another sip of her champagne, but it tasted just as foul as the first one. While the others were chattering, she slipped it onto a table behind her.

"Grace Trey," Kendra was saying. "Do you ever go by Gracie?"

"Sometimes, yeah."

"Gracie Trey," Kendra said to Larry. "Has a better ring to it, don't you think?"

He nodded. "I do."

"We're gonna have so much fun. I can hardly wait." Kendra beamed at Grace. "I'm not used to getting a star that's as naturally gorgeous as you." As she was going on about her plans, the waiter came by with his tray of champagne again. But Kendra just waved her hand. "I have no interest in glorified grape juice," she told him. "I'll have a vodka martini, three olives, please."

Grace couldn't help but be impressed—not only with Kendra's beauty and style but this was a woman who knew what she wanted and knew how to get it. Grace wondered if that was something she could learn. So sophisticated. So grown-up. Wouldn't that blow away everyone in Homewood. Particularly her dad. Well, on second thought, even a hundred-mile-an-hour hurricane couldn't blow that man away.

Grace was having such a good time at the Reynolds's mansion that she barely noticed that Renae Taylor hadn't shown up. Oh, well, there would be time for that. Besides, it might be nice if Grace had a little more confidence before her first encounter with her idol. Grace didn't want to embarrass herself any more than was necessary.

She was just coming back inside after admiring the city lights from the big back deck that overlooked a sapphire blue swimming pool. This place was to die for. She wondered if she'd ever become successful enough to buy a house like this. Maybe that would impress her dad. Although she doubted it.

Mossy was waving to her now. She went over to see what he wanted. "Something to show you," he said quietly. "But not out here."

She followed him into what looked like a library and waited as he handed her a large envelope with the Sapphire Music logo in the corner. "What is it?"

"Congratulations," he told her.

"Huh?" She started to open it.

"No, Gracie, don't open it here. That would be bad manners. Wait until you get home."

"Oh." She folded it to slide down into her small evening bag. "Okay."

"It's your first advance from Sapphire," he explained. "Should be enough for a car. And to get you by for a while."

"Really?" She fastened her bag securely closed. "Cool."

"You're on your way, Gracie Trey." He was leading her back out to where the other guests were visiting. The atmosphere seemed even louder and merrier than before.

She laughed happily. "This is like a really cool dream, Mossy. A totally cool dream. And if I'm dreaming, please, do not wake me up."

"While I have your attention," he said, "you're scheduled to record the single on Tuesday. Then on Wednesday you'll be with Kendra getting styled." He waved at someone across the room. "End of the week you'll be doing a showcase at—"

"Stop—stop," she told him. "My head is already spinning."

He laughed. "That's just the champagne."

"No, it's not." She frowned. "I barely touched it."

"Good. Johnny will be relieved to hear that."

"Are you reporting to Dad now?"

He solemnly shook his head. "I work for you, Gracie. Not your dad. And don't you forget it."

She shook her finger at him. "Don't you forget it either, Mr. Mossy." She sighed as she looked around the crowded room. "The only reason my head was spinning was because you were throwing too many dates and things and people at me. Can't you just have your assistant e-mail me a schedule or something?"

He chuckled. "Sure. That's exactly what I planned on doing. I was just trying to give you a little heads-up. Your career is taking off, Gracie Girl. Hold on for the ride." As if to make his point, he linked his arm in hers. "And now I want to go show you off to some of these fine people. Part of being here tonight is about being seen. So just play along with me, Gracie. Show these folks that you are a force to be reckoned with and that you are here to stay."

She looked up at him. "You really think so?"

He nodded. "I know so. I can feel it in my old bones."

She held her head high as Mossy led her around, working the room, and following his lead, she played the part of the up-and-coming musician. But by the time they finished, she felt a little tired of people making the continued reference to Johnny Trey. It was like they couldn't forget that she was his daughter. And the fact that she was redoing his record did not seem to help matters. She wondered if they would ever accept her for who she was—*Grace Trey* . . . rather *Gracie Trey*. Of course that only reminded her that in order to stand on her own two musical legs, she would be expected to write and record her own songs. The pressure was on.

# Chapter 11

**G**race couldn't wait to see the sound booth. She didn't know a lot about this kind of equipment, but she suspected it was all state-of-the-art and expensive. Sapphire Music wouldn't have settled for anything less. Mossy made sure they got there early enough to watch the tail end of another recording session. He felt it would be a good experience for Grace to see someone else recording. But she could hardly believe it when she saw that it was Tyson James and his band. Tyson was dressed casually in holey jeans, Converse, and a torn white T-shirt, but his long hair and multiple tattoos shouted "rocker" loud and clear.

"Want these?" A guy wearing a faded Stones T-shirt held out some headphones to her.

"Yeah," she whispered as if her voice might go beyond the soundproof glass.

She sat on the stool just soaking it all in as she listened and watched Tyson doing his final song for the day. It was even fun and educational to see the recording gurus doing their magic. And it actually looked pretty painless. They got it in the can after just three tries.

"Let's break," the guy who appeared to be in charge told everyone. He came over to greet Mossy. "So this is the girl?" He peered curiously at Grace. "Johnny's daughter—who would've thought."

"Yep." Mossy nodded. "This is Gracie Trey. Gracie, this is Bryant Stockwell. He's been doing this since before you were a glimmer in your mama's eye. And, trust me, no one does it better than Bryant."

Tyson and the band were coming out now, and Bryant must've seen the eager look in Grace's eyes. "You wanna go say hey?" he said to her.

She was unsure. "I don't want to look like a groupie."

They laughed, and then Mossy gave her a friendly push. "Go ahead. Rock stars don't bite."

"Not usually," Bryant teased.

She knew she looked nervous and totally starstruck as she introduced herself to Tyson, explaining why she was here. "I love your work," she said shyly. Fortunately, he didn't seem to mind her adoration.

"I've been a fan of your dad since I was a kid," he told her. "'Misunderstood' is still on my iPod."

"Cool." She nodded. "Hopefully you'll like my version of it too."

His eyes flickered up and down, as if he was really checking her out, and then he broke into a big grin. "I have a feeling I'll like it just fine."

She felt her cheeks warming. This was all so new . . . and weird . . . and cool.

"Good luck," he told her. "Break a leg in there." Then he chuckled and went off to join his band.

It took nearly an hour before everything was set up for her session, but she appreciated the extra time to get acquainted with the crew and acclimated to the studio. And to feel comfortable in her own skin. Her confidence level was high by the time she went into the sound booth and strapped on her guitar and adjusted her headphones. She could do this.

However, it wasn't long before she discovered that recording was hard work. In some ways it reminded her of rehearsing with the worship team—at first. But if she thought Dad was a stickler for detail, he was a teddy bear compared to Bryant Stockwell. Bryant was a Perfectionist with a capital P. By the end of the session, Grace wondered if Bryant suffered from OCD. Nothing—not a single thing—slipped past this man. They did so many takes of the song that she actually felt somewhat sick by the time they ended. Her ears were ringing and her head was throbbing.

"I think we got it," Bryant was telling Mossy when she went back to the engineering booth.

"That was harder than I expected," she confessed to them.

"It always is the first time." Bryant punched something into his computer. "But, don't worry, kid, you did fine. This is going to be a great single. Just wait and see."

"You're going to blow your dad's old song right out of the water," Mossy assured her.

On Wednesday morning Kendra Burroughs and another woman, loaded down with bags, showed up at Grace's apartment at ten. "This is my assistant Phoebe," Kendra explained. "And we need to do some measurements for wardrobe as well as get you ready for a photo shoot at two." She turned to Phoebe. "Wasn't I right? Isn't she gorgeous?"

With her finger on her chin, Phoebe nodded. "We could do so much with her."

"First things first. Get her measurements," Kendra told Phoebe.

As Phoebe measured and made notes, Kendra strolled around the little apartment, trying to decide which room had the best light. But Grace could tell by her expression that Kendra was unimpressed with Grace's new digs.

"You won't be living in the slums for long, Gracie." Kendra set what looked like a cosmetic case on the tiny dining table next to the window. "Not if you're as good as Mossy claims you are."

Before long Grace was seated at the table, and Kendra and Phoebe were applying makeup and commenting as if Grace wasn't even in the room.

"Should we have exfoliated her first?" Phoebe asked.

"No, her skin is flawless. Lucky girl."

"Are we going to change her hair color at all?"

"Larry said leave it blonde. It gives her wholesome appeal, which means that even parents will like her. Broadens the target market."

"We could always add some temporary streaks for concerts," Phoebe suggested. "Some hot pink or magenta would be fun."

"Sure, for concerts—that's when we want her to look like a hot little rocker chick. But not for the photo shoot."

"How 'bout this color for her lips?" Phoebe held up a tube of lipstick that looked slightly purplish. Not a shade Grace ever would've naturally been drawn to wear.

"Let's go for something more subtle." Kendra dug through the tray. "Like this." She handed Phoebe a lip liner in a pinkish shade. "Do a firm outline and then blend it," she told her. "With a layer of gloss on top. Larry said he wants her flirty—not trashy."

They both laughed as Phoebe worked on Grace's lips.

"How's that?" Phoebe said as she stepped back to look.

"Perfect." Kendra made a thumbs-up.

Phoebe nodded. "Yeah. It gives her a sense of innocence . . . but still enticing."

"Now for eyeliner." Kendra held up another tube. "You've got the steady hand, Phoebs, go for it." Kendra folded her arms, watching as Phoebe pulled out a thin brush.

"Close your eyes, doll," Phoebe told her.

Grace felt very much a like a doll as she closed her eyes, sitting still as something cool slid across her upper lids. Then Phoebe was blowing on them, and Grace had to hold her breath because Phoebe's breath was not the freshest.

"There," she said. "Open."

Kendra leaned down to peer at Grace and then firmly shook her head. "No, Phoebe, that's way too much. She looks too seductive."

"But I thought you said they wanted every red-blooded boy to love her. And every teenage girl to want to be like her?"

Kendra laughed. "But we want their mothers to love her too. We know she can look hot, but to start with we want *daddy's little girl* with an edge."

Grace cringed at that last comment but tried not to show it as Phoebe pulled a makeup remover wipe from the pack and started all over on her eyes. This time, not only did she apply more liner and eye shadow, but she curled Grace's eyelashes and put on what felt like a dozen layers of mascara.

"It's nice we don't need to use false eyelashes," she said as she put on the last coat. "How's that?"

"That'll work. Lashy but not trashy."

Again they laughed. And Grace attempted to join in, but somehow she was just not feeling it. She remembered how she used to protest about being Dad's puppet. What was she now? Still, she was determined not to go there. She knew this was just part of the deal—if you want to be a star, you have to look like a star. Get over it!

"When do I get to see?" Grace asked curiously.

"Not until we're done," Kendra said as she brushed something on her cheek.

When the makeup was finished, they pulled out the hair tools. Curling iron, flattening iron, and gels and sprays. Grace wanted to ask them what was wrong with a more natural look, but knew she needed to trust their judgment on this. After all, they were the pros.

"So for the photo shoot, we've brought some clothes," Kendra explained. "We know they won't fit exactly right, but we can adjust them with clothespins and stuff. We'll make it look right. When you do your showcase on Friday, we'll have real clothes that will fit perfectly."

"Cool." Grace smiled hopefully at Kendra. "Can I see it yet?"

"Sure." Kendra nodded. "Go take a peek, and we'll start figuring out what you'll wear for the shoot."

Grace went into the bathroom and turned on the light and then stared at her image in the mirror. Blinking, she looked again. This did not look like her. Not at all. What were they thinking? Was this some kind of joke? Feeling close to tears, she went back out to where they were laying out clothes and discussing which ones were right.

"Uh . . . I . . ." She held up her hands helplessly.

"What?" Kendra looked up from where she was playing with a denim jacket. "Something wrong?"

"My face," Grace said in a trembling voice. "It doesn't look like me."

"Of course, it looks like you," Kendra assured her. "Doesn't it, Phoebs?"

"Yeah. It's you." Phoebe nodded. "Only better."

"But . . . I—"

"Look," Kendra said gently, "we know this is all new to you. I guess we should've explained. Publicity shots have to look slick. Oh, they can Photoshop them up later, but we want to send you in there with just the right look." She held out her hands. "And you got it, babe. Trust me, you got it."

"Yeah, you look hot," Phoebe said. "And yet not too hot. You know?"

"And photography is funny," Kendra said. "It's like you need to overemphasize some things. What you're seeing in the bathroom, which I might add has really poor lighting, is nothing like what they'll be seeing in the photography studio where the lighting is hot and bright. Trust me, you will be thanking us later, Gracie."

"Oh," she let out a relieved sigh. "Okay, if you say so."

"We definitely say so." Phoebe held a pale pink shirt up to Grace now.

"No," Kendra said. "Too washed out. Try that darker one."

Suddenly Grace felt like a paper doll as Kendra and Phoebe held various ensembles up in front of her, taking turns to comment and critique. But eventually, they had five different outfits, complete with jewelry and accessories all ready to go.

"I'll start steaming and hanging these," Kendra said. "You pack the rest of it up." She pointed at Grace now. "You get yourself a little bite to eat. Not too much because it's never good to shoot on a full stomach, but enough to keep your blood sugar up. And drink a bottle of water too."

Grace went into the kitchen, feeling slightly like a child, but doing as she'd been told. She tried not to compare the way they were treating her to how she'd been treated at home, but it was impossible to ignore the similarities. Still, she told herself, this was what it took to get launched. The price all musicians must pay to succeed. Play along and, in time, the reward would come.

The photo shoot was similar to recording in that she had a professional crew telling her what to do and then having her do it again and again and again. The differences were, however, that she had to keep changing her clothes and hair—and although some shots included her guitar, she was not playing music. Still, she did her best to cooperate; and when they finally finished, everyone—including Mossy, who had watched the whole thing—seemed satisfied.

"You got some great shots," he told her as he drove her home. "Larry is going to like them. That Kendra really knows her stuff."

Grace tipped down the mirror behind the sun visor and peered at her strange-looking image. "You're sure I don't look overly made up?"

"Not at all. You have that fresh-faced, girl-next-door look."

She frowned at the painted eyes and lips. Girl next door to what?

The next day was relatively calm and quiet compared to the first part of the week. And Grace tried to use the time to write a song. But unfortunately it was just not coming to her. She knew she had no good excuse this time. Dad wasn't breathing down her neck. Mom wasn't expecting her to help out in the house. Rachel wasn't calling. The truth was, she wasn't distracted by anything more than the ticking of the clock, neighbors coming and going, and the occasional noises down on the street. And yet she was stuck.

On Friday afternoon, as scheduled, Kendra and Phoebe showed up at her apartment again. "Tonight you get to be *rocker chick*," Kendra said as she ceremoniously laid a black garment bag on the couch and set a pair of very cool-looking boots on the floor next to it. "Ready?"

Grace nodded, trying to exude more confidence than she felt. However those boots were pretty encouraging.

"Your throne," Phoebe said as she pulled out a dining room chair.

"Our goal for tonight is to make her look like less of a teen-ager," Kendra said to Phoebe. "For some reason teen singers make the night-club audience a little uncomfortable."

"Keeps her from getting carded too," Phoebe teased.

Grace sat quietly as the two went to work on her. It was similar to preparing for her photo shoot, although they seemed to be having more fun this time. And although she had no idea what she would look like when they finished, she knew there wasn't a whole lot she could do about it. Mossy had made that clear after the photo shoot. For the time being she belonged to Sapphire and Mossy. Go with the flow or just go.

"How about some magenta streaks," Phoebe asked when they started on her hair.

"Sure," Kendra agreed. "No more goody-good girl. We want her to be edgy tonight. Sell her to the twenty-to-thirty crowd."

After they finished hair and makeup, they didn't let her go look in the mirror. "Wait until you're dressed," Kendra insisted. "We want you to get the full effect."

Now Phoebe was unzipping the garment bag and removing what looked like a motorcycle jacket, except that it was brown not black.

"At first I thought this was too cliché," Kendra told Grace. "But on second thought, I think it's perfect. We needed something to give you a rocker's edge."

"What do you think?" Phoebe asked Grace.

Grace fingered the soft leather then nodded. "I really like it."

The women seemed relieved. And before long Grace was completely dressed in rocker style. The jacket felt great and she loved the boots.

"Go ahead and look now," Kendra said.

Instead of going to the bathroom, Grace went into the bedroom where there was a full-length mirror on the closet door. When she saw her reflection, she couldn't help but laugh.

"Hey, what's so funny?" Kendra asked as she came into the bedroom to see.

"Me." Grace was laughing so hard she was doubled over.

"You are not funny," Phoebe said from behind Kendra. "You are hot."

"Stand up straight," Kendra commanded. "Act like the rocker chick we know you are."

"Here," Phoebe handed Grace her guitar case. "Maybe you need a prop."

So Grace got out her guitar and strapped it on and struck a rocker pose in front of the mirror. "Wow!" She blinked in surprised. "I do look like a rocker chick."

They both laughed.

"Of course you do," Kendra declared.

"That's what we were going for," Phoebe pointed out.

Grace didn't want to think what her family and friends would say if they could see her like this. She knew that the church congregation would be scratching their heads too. But those were not the people who would be listening to her tonight. No, she told herself, this was a whole different world. And the sooner she got comfortable in this world, the sooner she would succeed in it.

## Chapter 12

Grace (aka *Gracie*) wound up doing three showcase venues within a week's time. Although it had started out exciting, Grace could tell she was becoming jaded. Maybe *jaded* was the wrong word. But she was skeptical. She didn't mention her concerns to anyone, not even Mossy, but as she was getting ready for her fifth showcase, in yet another LA club, she felt seriously doubtful.

"Let's give her big hair tonight," Phoebe was telling Kendra. "With blue highlights to go with that top."

Kendra seemed to consider this as she paused to sip a cocktail that she'd brought backstage with her. She and Phoebe always seemed to have alcohol on hand. "Yeah." Kendra nodded. "Blue highlights. It'll be fun."

As usual Grace kept her opinions to herself as she took a drink from her water bottle. What did it matter if she had blue, green, or purple highlights? And what good did it do to get up there and sing her dad's one-hit wonder to a crowd that was obviously there to drink and hook up? Oh, sure, they clapped and cheered. But then they went back to their drinking and dancing and flirting; Grace felt certain she was forgotten.

"Use this lip color," Kendra told Phoebe as she held the shiny tube to the light so she could read the bottom. "Purple Plum Madness." She laughed. "Yummy."

Grace held her lips slightly apart, like she'd been trained to do while Phoebe slathered on the lipstick. She wondered when she'd get to play for an audience that had actually come to see her. Would fans ever buy tickets just because they were into her music? Or would she be always playing in second-rate clubs like this one? She'd seen an actual rat outside the backstage door tonight, and it was at least a foot long!

As the stylists continued with her hair and makeup, Grace tried not to remember the e-mail she'd gotten from her mom this morning. Mom tried to sound brave and encouraging, but Grace could read between the lines. Mom was freaking. When she told Grace she was keeping her in her prayers "both day and night," Grace knew that meant Mom was waking in the middle of the night, worrying about her. Probably having a maternal panic attack. But, Grace reassured herself as she was pulling on a new pair of boots, even if she was safely tucked away at college, her mom would still be worried. That was what parents did. Grace hadn't answered the e-mail yet, wasn't sure if she even would. Really, what could she say?

"Ready to rock and roll?" Kendra gave Grace's hair one more fluff and a spray.

"Sure." Grace gave them a forced smile, avoiding looking into the well-lit dressing room mirror. She'd learned that hard lesson last week. It was better not to know exactly how she looked before she went out on stage. Perhaps in time she'd get used to the harsh makeup and overly styled hair. But she just wasn't there yet.

Still, as she took her guitar out of its case, she felt the usual comfort of holding such a familiar part of her life . . . her old life. She stroked the smooth wood finish and sighed. Some day she'd be able to call the shots. Until then she would keep jumping through these hoops.

"Ready to go?" the stage manager called into the room.

"I'm coming." Grace thanked her faithful stylists. And they held up their drink glasses and, using language her parents would not approve of, told her to go out and rock the house.

And rock the house, she did. The only time Grace truly felt like herself was when she was performing, when she was moving and singing and playing and rocking. Now that felt good! For the length of the song, she could pretend the audience was there to see her. And she could pretend everything in her life was on track. She could even pretend being made up and dressed up and paraded around like a circus monkey was okay. But then the song ended, and it was time to face reality again.

"Great job," Mossy said as he greeted her backstage. "You look hot, and your performance was on fire. The crowd loved you."

She shrugged. "I guess."

"Hey, what's with the glum face?"

She made a stiff smile. "Sorry. I guess I just keep hoping I'll get a gig where people really come to see me."

"That's what we're working toward," he reminded her. "This is paying your dues."

"I know. I know." She tried to brighten up her smile. She didn't want him to think she was ungrateful. "Maybe I'm just tired."

"And just you wait until that single comes out—then they are going to be all over you. That's when everything'll change. You just gotta be patient till then, Gracie. A rock star isn't built in a day. You do wanna be a star, don't you?"

Her smile grew more genuine now. "Absolutely." She nodded.

He slapped her on the back. "Good girl. Now go on out there and schmooze with your fans while I talk to the club manager for a few minutes. Need to attend to some business."

So Grace went back out to the crowded club where she always tried to act like she was comfortable but never really quite fit in. Sure, a few people would greet her. And almost on cue, some drunk dude would come hit on her. But she really did not understand why people found this atmosphere so enjoyable.

"Over here!" Kendra called out over the loud music.

Relieved to see a familiar face, she went over and joined Kendra at a tall table. "You were fabulous tonight," Kendra told Grace. "Really, you had these guys eating out of your hand."

"Thanks!"

"Now if you just had more songs to give 'em, I'll bet they would keep you up there all night." Kendra waved to a waiter now, holding up two fingers and nodding.

"I'm working on more songs," Grace told her.

"Good for you. Because with talent like yours, you shouldn't waste it on a single. You know what I mean?"

Grace smirked at her. "You mean like my dad?"

Kendra threw back her head and laughed. "Well, I didn't want to name names."

Now the waiter came to their table, and after complimenting Grace on her performance, he plunked down two pink cocktails then took off.

"Who's the other one for?" Grace asked.

"For you," Kendra told her. "Let's drink to your success."

Grace studied the drink for a moment.

"Come on, Gracie. It'll do you good. Might loosen you up a little. You seem pretty uptight, you know."

Grace reached for the drink and took a tentative sip. "That's not bad," she told Kendra. "Better than champagne."

Kendra winked at her. "I thought you'd like it."

The following Friday Grace was doing another showcase appearance at another club. But by now she was getting resolved to this crazy lifestyle. Like Mossy kept telling her, she was paying her dues. But she was also getting a little more confidence. Besides that, the single was about to release. And already she'd seen posters with her face on them. It was actually starting to happen, and it was exciting.

"How about a little less *Early Avril Lavigne*," she said to Kendra as they started getting ready backstage. "And a little more *Post Renae Tyler* for my look tonight?"

Kendra laughed. "You saying you want us to soften you up some?"

"Just for a change," Grace suggested.

"Sure." Kendra took a sip of her martini. "Why not?"

"But if Moss complains, you gotta take the heat," Phoebe warned.

"No problem," she assured them. "I'm a big girl."

Tonight, when they finished with her, she actually did look in the mirror and, to her relieved surprise, she looked okay.

Better than okay—she looked good. "Thanks, you guys," she told the pair.

"Go rock 'em!" Kendra held up her glass.

"Knock 'em dead," Phoebe called out.

Feeling more assured than ever, she took the stage by storm and launched into what she felt was one of her strongest performances. She just wished that it could go on and on. She needed more songs!

Afterward, she went out to the club to look for Mossy. She wanted to hear his reaction to her softened-up appearance as well as her heated-up performance. When she spotted Moss, he was sitting with a guy who looked exactly like TV superstar Jay Grayson. And the closer she got to their table, the more this dude looked like Grayson.

"There she is," Mossy said loudly above the music. "Gracie Trey, I want you to meet Jay Grayson."

For a split second she was speechless, but not wanting to look like the starstruck dimwit that she really was, she stuck out her hand and smiled. "Pleasure to meet you, Jay Grayson." She could feel her knees trembling, but at least she was still standing upright.

"You too, Gracie." His eyes lit up. "Hey, Grayson and Gracie—that kinda has a nice ring to it."

She laughed as Mossy pulled out a stool for her.

"You were great out there," Jay told her. "Really awesome."

"Thanks."

"Mossy tells me you're still new to Hollywood, but you could've fooled me. You look like you're fitting in just fine."

"I'm learning the ropes." She elbowed Mossy. "Paying my dues."

He winked. "That's right. Everybody does it."

Jay nodded. "Yep. I paid mine too."

"So how do you know Mossy?" she asked. "Are you a musician as well as an actor?"

"No. But my brother Drew is a musician, and Moss reps him."

"Aha." She gave Mossy a sly look. "And here you had me thinking I was your only client."

He laughed. "That's what I want all my clients to think. Makes you feel special."

"Better watch out for that one," Jay warned in a teasing tone.

Grace could tell that some of the club patrons were watching their table and whispering among themselves. She knew that was mostly because of Jay, but she pretended that it was because of her too. It wouldn't be long now—people would be turning their heads to notice Gracie Trey just as much as Jay Grayson. The fun was just beginning. She could feel it.

Just a few days later everything she'd dreamed of seemed like it was finally happening. It started with Mossy dropping by several promotional posters for her at the apartment. "They turned out real nice," he said as he unfurled one to show her.

"Wow!" She stared at the image of herself on the glossy Sapphire Music poster. "This is so cool!"

"I brought you some extras in case you wanna send some home."

"Sure. Thanks!" She wondered what her parents would think if she sent them one . . . or Rachel. For all she knew, they would probably think she was flaunting herself or bragging. They might even use the posters for fire starter.

"And I assume you have a radio," Mossy said with a twinkle in his eye.

"The single is out?"

"Some early releases are going out to the radio stations this afternoon." He told her some station numbers to tune in to. "You'll want to be listening this evening."

"You bet. Absolutely."

After Mossy left, she turned on the radio, listening to songs by performers she admired as she straightened up her apartment. Then she tried her poster on several walls, finally settling on a good spot in the living room behind the couch. She was just looking for something to stick it onto the wall with when a song by Renae Tyler started to play. She danced to the music as she went through the kitchen drawers, where to her surprise, she found some pushpins. Mossy's assistant seemed to have thought of most everything.

With Renae still singing, Grace climbed onto the couch to hang the poster. She was putting in the last pin as the song ended, and she could hear the DJ speaking in the usual fast-talking DJ sort of way, but it was the mention of her dad's name that caught her attention. She hopped down from the couch and listened.

"Well his daughter did her own version, and I got to tell you, this girl can really sing! Here's the premiere of Gracie Trey singing her daddy's hit, 'Misunderstood.'"

Grace started jumping around the apartment like a crazy girl now. She was so excited, she wanted to call someone. But at the same time she just wanted to listen to the song. Hopping up and down, she was laughing and crying and carrying on so wildly that she got worried the people in the apartment below might call in a complaint. The song ended, and she flopped down onto the couch. This was it. She had made it. Wow.

She sat there for awhile, just trying to soak it all in, longing for the moment to last longer. And then, even more than that, she longed to share it with someone. She could call Mossy, but that seemed anticlimactic since he's the one who told her it would be on. She could call the stylists, but this wasn't big news in their world.

She picked up her phone and considered calling Rachel. But after their last conversation she was pretty sure it would end up being another downer or a lecture about being a good daughter. And her parents, well, that was just out of the question.

Johnny was sitting at his computer when Michelle came up from behind him. Tempted to close it before she read the headline, he knew that would only make her more suspicious. And so he just left it open.

"Did she survive?" Michelle asked stiffly.

"I, uh, I didn't finish the article."

Michelle leaned over his shoulder, reading aloud. "Rising young actress Jessica Skeens, brutally assaulted outside her Los Angeles apartment, remains in critical—"

He closed the lid shut with a snap.

"Sounds like she's still alive," Michelle said in a flat voice.

"I'm sorry," Johnny let out a sad sigh.

"Sorry she's alive?"

"No, of course not. Sorry you had to see that."

"Well, apparently *you* had to see that." Michelle came around to face him now. "How long are you gonna do this, John? Are you gonna find every story about a girl who gets hurt in Hollywood?"

He shoved the laptop aside. "I miss her."

"Well, so do I." She tipped her head toward his computer. "And, believe me, my heart breaks for this poor Jessica girl, and I will be praying for her family. But what does her story have to do with our Grace? Why do you keep going there?"

Johnny just sat there, drumming his fingers and trying to come up with a logical answer. Problem was, there was none. Logic had nothing to do with it.

"I should go," he told her in a sharp voice.

"Tell Tim hello." Michelle's voice sounded flat and lifeless.

As Johnny left the house, he knew they weren't handling this right. But how were they supposed to handle it? He felt as if they were grieving. And yet Grace wasn't dead. In some ways it would almost be easier if she were dead. Johnny hated feeling that way, but it was true. Having her gone from her lives like this—well, it was just too painful. *Maybe it was like divorce,* he thought as he drove to the coffee shop to meet Pastor Tim. He'd heard divorced wives say that they would've preferred if their husbands had died rather than cheated on them. Maybe that was how he and Michelle felt. Except that he would never—never in a million years—wish his daughter dead. But the truth was it would probably be easier.

Pastor Tim was already waiting as Johnny carried his coffee over to the table. They exchanged the usual pleasantries, and then Tim asked how he was doing. Johnny tried to be as truthful as he dared with him, but not wanting to break down in public, he didn't say everything that was tumbling through his heart.

"And Michelle?" Tim asked gently. "How's she holding up?"

"She has her good days and bad—we both do."

"Of course. So what's the latest with your album?"

Johnny knew that Tim was graciously attempting to move on to a more comfortable subject. If that was possible. "Still on hold," Johnny admitted. "Can't bring myself to do it. Just doesn't feel right. It's hard enough getting up in front of the church every week." He shook his head dismally and took another sip of his black coffee.

"You know what kills me," he continued. "It's that I'm responsible for all this. It was my old song, my manager. . . ." He ran his hand through his hair. "And, sure, having my music in front of millions was a dream come true for me. But you better know where to draw the line. You better be grounded. I wasn't . . . and neither is Grace."

Tim just shook his head. "God can bring good things out of evil, Johnny."

"But I honestly thought I could somehow protect her from all of that. At least until I thought she was ready. . . . Obviously, I failed."

"You and Shelly are good parents, Johnny. Sure, you're not perfect. None of us are. But this isn't about that. You can't keep blaming yourself."

Johnny wanted to believe Tim, but it was just too hard. "We call her," he said. "E-mail, text her. Tell her we love her. Tell her we're praying for her. But my own daughter won't even talk to me."

"That's gotta be tough." Tim just shook his head. "You think that's how God feels sometimes?"

Johnny considered this. "It can't be easy being God, can it? Just think how many kids He's got who aren't talking to Him." He almost added, "including my daughter," but stopped himself. Because, really, what good did it do to keep tearing her down? Especially seeing how she seemed to be doing a pretty good job of that herself.

# Chapter 13

When Grace deposited her first advance check from Sapphire, it had felt like winning the lottery. As a result she'd been enjoying the luxury of spending freely. If she wanted something, she simply bought it. It was awesome. However, she did have this underlying feeling that she should be more careful with her money. Having grown up in a frugal family, she knew what it was like to go without. When they were doing the church circuit, they got by on "whatever the Lord provided." Sometimes it was mac and cheese and cheap hotels. Other times it was better.

*Today was a lot better,* she thought, as she carried her grocery bags out to her car. No mac and cheese for this girl. She wondered what Mom would think of the foods she'd purchased just now. Not that she'd gone for junky things like chips and sodas. No way. She was in LA, and people here cared about healthy nutrition. Her bags were filled with granola and soy milk and Greek yogurt and pomegranate juice and all sorts of things

Kendra and Phoebe had recommended. And, sure, she tossed in a package of Oreos too. Just for balance.

She was putting them in the back of the car just as her phone started to ring. Checking it first, as she ran around to the driver's seat, to make sure it wasn't her parents, she breathlessly answered. "Hey, Moss! What's up?"

"Hey, Gracie girl, what're you doing?"

"Grocery shopping," she said as she tossed her purse onto the glossy photo book Mossy had given her yesterday. The book contained samples of the famed photographer Randall Preston. Apparently Mr. Preston preferred shooting his models in the buff. Embarrassed to be seen with such a book and not wanting it in her apartment, she'd intentionally left it in her car.

"Yeah, well, it's good to eat," he said. But something about the tone of his voice sounded more serious than usual.

"Something wrong?" She put her keys into the ignition.

"Oh, well. It's a little early to tell, I think."

"What?"

"I don't want to worry you, Gracie, but the single has gone flat."

She took in a quick breath—was it over already? "Flat?" she repeated. "What do you mean *flat?*"

"It happens. Airplay's good. It's just the downloads. They're slow this week. That's all."

Gracie looked at her new car, trying not to consider how much it had set her back or how long she could get by on what remained in her bank account. Why hadn't she been more frugal? "So, what do we do now?" she asked nervously.

"Relax. This is normal."

"The video will help—*right?*"

"Of course. Don't get all freaked out."

But she was freaked out. The word flat kept reverberating around in her head, attaching itself to other words. Flat tire. Flat line. *Flat broke.* None of it sounded encouraging.

"Really, Gracie, I got it under control. You don't need to worry. You just worry about your follow-up song, okay? When are we gonna hear it?"

"I . . . uh . . . I'm almost ready." She shut her eyes tightly, as if she could block out the lie. "I want it just right, you know?"

"Sapphire just wants a demo, Gracie. It doesn't have to be perfect."

*New subject*, she was thinking as she pushed the grocery receipt into her purse. Then, seeing the skanky photo album, she decided to go there. "So I looked though Randall's photos."

"He's amazing, isn't he?"

"The girls aren't wearing anything."

"Oh, come on, that's not true. Sure, there's a little skin, but it's classy. And when you start charting, we're gonna need some killer photos. He's the best there is, Gracie. We'd be lucky to get him."

"Yeah, I don't know." She flipped through some pages, then closed the book and put her purse back over it.

"He's going to shoot Renae Taylor's next cover."

She considered this. *"Really?"*

"Of course. I'm telling you, Randall's our guy. You're a beautiful girl, Gracie. Let's make the most of it."

She pulled down the visor mirror and peered up at herself. At least she looked like herself today. No excessive makeup or overdone hair.

"Hey, I just remembered something. Jay Grayson's manager called. Apparently Jay wants to take you out."

She flipped the visor up. *"What?"*

"Apparently when Jay met you, according to his manager, you *charmed* him." Mossy chuckled.

*"Really?"*

"Jay's words, not mine. Well, his manager's anyway."

"And you were going to tell me this—*when?*"

"Hey, I just did."

They chatted awhile longer, and then Moss said he had to go tend to business. Grace started her car and drove toward her apartment. Of course, as she was driving, her mind was in a world of its own—her first date with Jay Grayson. What would she say to him? "Hey, Jay, cool to see you again. Been looking forward to this," she said aloud, as if he was with her. No way, she shook her head as she pulled into her parking space. Too corny. She tried it again. "So, how exactly did I *charm* you?"

she would say coyly—putting him on the spot. Yeah, she liked that line. As she went upstairs, she tried another. "You know, this may sound weird," she began as she slid her key into the door. "But I can *always* tell when a guy—" She stopped herself and looked at the door. Was it ajar?

Feeling uneasy, she looked around, trying to remember if the door had been cracked open or if she'd just been too involved in her daydream to notice. Probably the latter. And yet the hair on the back of her neck was sticking out. And her heart was pounding.

"Hello?" She called out as she pushed the door wide open. "Anyone in there?" Holding her grocery bags like a shield in front of her, she stepped inside the apartment and called again. Now she noticed that her bedroom door was open and the light was on. Had she left it like that? It was possible, but she really couldn't remember. She waited and listened but heard nothing. Even so, this was enough to creep her out. She was not staying in here another moment until someone checked it out for her.

Hurrying for the door, with her bags still in her arms, she burst out of her apartment, colliding with someone who seemed to be coming in. The bag containing her produce split open, and she let out a startled scream.

"Easy there," the stranger told her as he stepped into the apartment and set a tote bag down inside the door. "Didn't mean to startle you."

*"Who are you?"* Holding up a bottle of Paul Newman balsamic vinegar salad dressing as a weapon, she did a quick study of the intruder. Tall, well built, good looking, neatly dressed, probably not much older than her. Not exactly the profile of a criminal, but who knew?

"You just get home?" he calmly asked from within her apartment—like he thought he belonged there. "First time round I knocked, like ten times, I promise. No one—"

*"Who are you?"* She swung the salad dressing menacingly toward his handsome face. *"Get out!"*

"Hey, easy there. I'm Quentin. I'm interning with Sapphire. Kendra had me drop off some clothes, I think . . . for your video." He nudged the nylon tote bag with his toe.

"How'd you get in?" she demanded, still on guard.

He kneeled to pick up her scattered fruits and vegetables. Gathering a melon, English cucumbers, pomegranates, and a bag of kale into his arms, he carried them over to the dining table and set them down. Not exactly the act of a serial killer, or so she hoped.

"The office gave me a key," he said as he returned for a second load. "They weren't sure you'd be here."

"Well, you could've called!" Still feeling shocked, she cautiously came into the apartment, leaving the door open behind her, just in case. Meanwhile Quentin, if that was his real name, was setting the remainder of her produce on the table. For a moment their eyes locked, and he gave her a funny expression—almost as if he was slightly starstruck. Then, with a mango still in hand, he went over to get the tote bag he'd been carrying during their collision. She eyed the bag suspiciously, thinking it could contain anything—guns, knives, ropes—although she didn't think so.

With his eyes still fixed on her, Quentin absent-mindedly dropped the mango into the bag and then carried it over to her. "Anyway, this is the last of it," he said with what seemed a little less confidence than before. "And I—I hung the rest in your closet. Hope that's okay."

She peered down into the tote bag and, seeing that it actually did contain clothing, she felt reassured. This Quentin dude was legit. And he was cute. She removed the misplaced mango and held it up. "So, am I supposed to wear this for the video?"

"Huh?" He looked blankly at the fruit. "What's that?"

"A mango." She suppressed the urge to laugh.

"What?" He made a sheepish smile.

"Is that supposed to be an accent to go with this ruffled cami?" she teased. "Or maybe I should wear it on a hat with some bananas and grapes?"

Quentin chuckled and Grace couldn't help but smile.

"Yeah, that's probably not going to work. I don't think they want you looking like Carmen Miranda."

"Carmen who?"

"You don't watch old flicks?" He sounded surprised. "Carmen Miranda was the rage in the fifties. She's the one who wore the fruity hats."

"Oh, yeah." She studied him curiously now, trying to wrap her head around an attractive guy who delivered clothes to girls' apartments and knew about movie stars from more than sixty years ago. Very interesting.

"Sorry to scare you like that," he said as he went for the door. "But it is good to be wary of strangers in this town."

She nodded. "Point taken."

"So . . . see you around." He gave her one more smile. "And don't forget to lock your door."

As she went to lock the door, it irked her to know that she wasn't the only one to have a key to her apartment. She'd have to ask Mossy about that. As she snapped the dead bolt into place, she remembered with amusement how Quentin had dropped the mango in with her clothes.

"It's all set," Mossy told her on Thursday morning.

"What's all set?" She laid her guitar on the couch, giving her full attention to the phone.

"Your date with Jay."

"*What date?*" She felt a mixture of excitement and angst. Was this really happening?

"Remember I told you that Jay was *charmed* by you? That he wanted to go out with you?"

"Yeah."

"Well, it's all set."

"Seriously?" She sank into a chair, trying to absorb Mossy's words. She was going out on a date? For real? She'd never been on a date before, and now she was going out with Jay Grayson! It seemed impossible and wonderful—and totally crazy. How would she know how to act? What to say? What to do?

"I thought you'd be excited."

"Of course, I'm excited. But I'm also a little shocked. And why isn't he calling me himself?"

Mossy laughed. "Jay is a busy boy, Gracie. He's probably filming right now. Do you want him to ask everyone on the set to take a break so that he can call—"

"Yeah, yeah, I get it."

"Anyway, tonight's the big night. Jay will pick you up around seven-thirty or eight."

"What kind of date is this?"

"A dinner date, of course."

"Why does everyone eat dinner so late here?"

He laughed. "You'll get used to it, Gracie, in time."

"Okay, so how do I dress?" she asked, thinking maybe it was a good thing Moss had set this up. That way she could ask all the questions she wanted.

"You dress to kill," he said.

"Really?"

"Oh, yeah, baby. This is a big night. A date with Jay Grayson. You want to look like the rock star you are—make an entrance."

"I thought you said this was a date." She frowned. "Am I going to have to sing for my supper?"

He laughed. "You can be so funny sometimes."

"Seriously, what do I wear? Like a dress? Like going to a cocktail party at the Reynolds's?"

"Exactly. Like a party at the Reynolds's. You get the picture."

"Thanks, Moss."

"Have fun tonight, Gracie."

"Yeah, if I can get past these nerves, I'll try."

After she hung up, Grace considered calling Kendra for some fashion advice, but knowing that Kendra would probably want to overdo it, Grace decided to just go with her instincts. Besides, after these past few weeks, she'd learned a thing or two. She could put herself together without help tonight.

Of course, her focus on getting ready for her date completely derailed her from working on that "next song." Not that she'd been having any success. As usual, she seemed to be suffering from songwriter's block.

Grace was ready for her big date by seven. But as the hands on the clock slowly moved, it became seven-thirty. She anxiously looked out the window to the street, trying not to see the church and the cross, hoping to spy a cool car since she was certain he would be driving a very cool car. But as it got closer to eight, her stomach was growling, and she was just heading for the kitchen to grab a quick bite to ward off her hunger, when she heard someone knocking at her door. She looked through the peephole to see him standing there, Mr. Hollywood, looking completely out of place in front of her shabby apartment. Why hadn't she thought to just meet him somewhere.

"Hey," she said as she opened the door. "Welcome to my world." She made a goofy smile. "Hopefully it won't be my world for long."

He shrugged. "It's okay. I used to live in a dump like this too."

She tried not to react to the word *dump*.

"You ready to go?"

She nodded. "Oh, yeah." She wanted to add she was starving but didn't think that sounded quite right. Instead, she asked how his day had gone, and he immediately launched into a story about how everything went wrong on the set.

"I've had a call into my manager since this afternoon. I can't believe he hasn't returned my call." He led her to a beautiful Porsche convertible parked in the visitors' section and opened the door. "Our ride."

"This is a gorgeous car, Jay." She slid onto the leather seat and looked around, taking in all the electronic gear on the dash. Way more options than her car had.

"Thanks. Just one of the little perks of success." He turned to smile at her from the driver's seat. "You'll get there too, Gracie. I can tell."

She smiled and relaxed a little. "I sure hope so."

Now he started talking about his journey to success and, although it took the pressure off of her, she couldn't help but feel like she was watching a documentary on the life and achievements of Jay Grayson. And then she felt like slapping herself—was she crazy? Here she was riding through Hollywood in a gorgeous car with the even more gorgeous Jay Grayson seated next to her, and she was inwardly grousing about it. Really, she had to be nuts! Or maybe she was just hungry.

# Chapter 14

After her little lecture to herself, Grace forced herself to relax and play the attentive and adoring date. Who cared if Jay liked to talk about himself? And, really, it was interesting. And educational. Everyone in Hollywood had come from somewhere else. All of them had stories to tell. She could learn a lot from people like Jay. And he was hot!

When he pulled up to the swanky restaurant, she felt like she was playing a scene in a movie. The sun was just going down as not one, but two, valets hurried up to the car. One opened her door and helped her out. The other greeted Jay like an old buddy and took the keys to his car. Then, as if on cue, several paparazzi snapped photos of the two of them walking into the restaurant together. She felt like royalty. Oh, sure, someday she might resent having people snapping photos of her right and left. But that day was not here yet.

With her arm linked in Jay's, she held her head high and, feeling like she was on top of the world, followed the maître d' into a private lounge, which apparently was only for celebrities. Nice. They were barely there and seated when Jay's phone buzzed. He excused himself, holding up his phone. "Gotta take this," he said.

"No problem," she said calmly. More than anything she wanted to appear poised and at ease. This may not have been her world before, but it was becoming her world now. She'd do everything she could to *make* it her world. She looked down at the cocktail dress she'd chosen for the evening. "A little bit classy and a little bit sassy," is how Kendra described it when she'd shown it to her. Perfect, Grace decided as she leaned back and listened to the background music. It was a nice bluesy jazz number, sophisticated and smooth. Just right for the atmosphere.

She thought about where she'd been just a few months ago—as good as she'd been at daydreams, she never would have imagined she'd be here now. And with Jay Grayson! Really, it was a dream come true. She thought about pulling out her own phone right now, snapping a photo of herself, and shooting off a text to Rachel. Except that she could imagine Rachel's response: (1) She'd be horrified that Grace was in a lounge. (2) She'd probably think Grace's dress was to risqué. And (3) she'd probably say something snarky about Jay Grayson. No, this was just one more amazing moment that Grace would have to keep to herself.

"Sorry about that," Jay said as he rejoined her. "My manager freaks if I don't take his call." He rolled his eyes as he dropped his phone back in his pocket. "Although he sure takes his time to answer mine."

"No worries," she smiled, resisting the urge to pinch herself.

"So what are you drinking?"

Grace considered this. Although she'd accepted several by now, from Kendra and Phoebe, she'd never actually ordered her own drink before. And she didn't consider herself a drinker. Not that she wanted Jay to know that. More than anything she wanted to impress him. She wanted to make him believe that she fit in here with him—that she wasn't really a hick. Suddenly she remembered Kendra's favorite drink. "I'll have a vodka martini," she said with fake confidence, "with three olives."

"Nice." Jay smiled as he waved to the bartender who looked up eagerly. "Hey, Bobby, the little lady will have a Cîroc-tini, three olives. And get me a Black Bull."

"You got it, Jay."

Now Jay turned his attention back on her. "So . . . Gracie Trey, thanks for hanging out with me."

She felt her heart flutter a little. "Oh, my pleasure."

"You know that ever since your show last week, I haven't stopped thinking about you."

Okay, it took all her self-control not to leap to her feet and launch into a Snoopy happy dance right now. Instead, she took in a deep breath and just smiled. "Wow."

He nodded. "Yeah, wow. So, tell me, Gracie Trey, what do you do when you're not rocking the house? Tell me about the *real* Gracie Trey."

And finally it was her turn to talk, but the problem was she really didn't have much to say. Who was the real Gracie Trey? Did he mean her childhood? Because no way was she going to tell him about how she grew up hopping from church to church, playing her dad's musical sidekick and puppet, sitting quietly on a pew while he told the story of how he'd thrown his life away as a troubled musician. She wasn't going to tell him about eating cheap fast food and wearing secondhand clothes. And she didn't want to talk about how she'd been on the worship team at church or how she could never do anything right in her dad's eyes. Really, it seemed so much easier just to make stuff up—sure, mix in enough truth to make it believable.

So she told him about her childhood and how they spent so much time on the road because of her dad's music. But instead of calling it a "ministry" like Dad always did, she called it a "career." She described how her dad taught her to play guitar and piano when she was little. She even told him about how she was the rock star in her church but how she wanted more. She told him that she'd been writing a really great song this week. "For my next release," she explained. "Mossy thinks Sapphire will want me to do an album."

"And you will." He raised his glass to her. "To your big break and a big album, Gracie Trey. And the one after that and the one after that."

Mossy was pacing back and forth, rubbing his chin and trying to come up with a good angle. An angle he could sell to Sally. He and Sally Benson of WideSpin were meeting in a Sapphire conference room, and for some reason—probably just because she could—Sally was being cantankerous. He'd known Sally for nearly thirty years, and to say she was jaded about the music business was definitely an understatement. And yet she made her living reporting on the goings-on of the music industry. Rather the gossip.

"Look," he said. "Don't forget who gave you the tip in the first place."

She frowned up from her laptop. "What are you saying, Moss? Don't you *like* the layout? Keep in mind, it's just a mock-up. But you gotta admit the photo of Jay and Gracie is priceless. Very *provocative*."

"The photo is good, and I'm glad Gracie never figured it out." He pointed to her computer screen. "But the headline. I thought we agreed you'd include Gracie's name."

She scowled at him. "Hey, for a guy who hasn't had a hit in a decade, you're awfully pushy."

"And you wouldn't have an exclusive if it wasn't for me."

She pursed her bright red lips, then nodded. "Fair enough."

Mossy smiled. "Plus, this girl's gonna get me back on the map."

"Speaking of the girl, I thought you said she was meeting us here today."

"She's on her way. Kendra picked her up."

As Grace and Kendra entered the Sapphire lobby, Kendra continued to quiz Grace on her date with Jay.

"I still can't believe you didn't call me for fashion advice." Kendra made a pout face.

"I thought you said you liked what I chose for the date."

"Yeah, well, I would've liked to have had a say in it too." Kendra pushed the up button for the elevator.

Grace laughed. "Okay, next time."

"Aha, so there's a next time."

"I didn't say—"

"But you want to go out with him again, don't you?" Kendra led the way into the elevator, which was thankfully empty except for them. Grace wasn't exactly ready to go public with her relationship with Jay Grayson. If it even was a relationship. "You do, don't you?" Kendra pushed the button for the conference room floor.

Grace held up her hands helplessly. "Yeah, maybe, I don't know."

Kendra chuckled. "That's what I like—a girl who really knows her mind. So, tell me, what else did you do on your fabulous date?"

"Mostly we just laughed a lot. We talked and talked and talked." Grace sighed. "Oh, Kendra, he was such a gentleman. It was just so much fun."

"All right, I'm officially jealous," Kendra declared as they emerged from the elevator.

"Oh, please, you can get any guy."

"It's getting the *right* guy that's the problem. Now back to you and Jay. When are you going out again?" she asked as they walked down the long hallway to the conference room.

"I don't know." Grace bit her lip. "Think I should call him?"

"No way. Let him call you. After all, you're Gracie Trey."

"That's right." Grace struck a rock star pose in front of the conference room door. "I'm Gracie Trey."

Kendra chuckled. "Yeah. It's all about the attitude."

Grace frowned at the door. "I know we're running late," she said quietly. "Think I have time to use the restroom?"

"You're Gracie Trey," Kendra said with an amused smile. "Ms. Sally Benson can wait."

Grace giggled as she hurried back down the hall to the bathroom. She was trying not to feel nervous about this meeting, but meeting Sally for the first time was a bit over-whelming. She'd been reading her blog for ages, and now Sally wanted to talk to Grace. It was just too much. Grace was just imagining what she'd say to Sally as she pushed open the rest-room door. In the same moment someone came barreling out, nearly knocking her down. To her confused surprise it was the same guy who'd scared the stuffing out of her at her apartment the other day—the intern from Sapphire.

"What are you doing in there?" she demanded hotly. First he breaks into her apartment, and now he's hanging in the women's restroom—what was wrong with this dude?

"Uh," he pointed to the sign on the door. "It's the men's room."

Her eyes grew wide as she read the sign. "Well, of course it is." She made a wimpy smile. "Sorry about that."

"Is this gonna be a pattern?" He sounded like he was try-ing to make a joke. "I mean bumping into each other—not . . . uh, the men's room." He waved his hand as if to erase his bad joke. "Never mind."

Without answering, she gave him a curious look before she asked herself, *What am I doing out here chatting with an intern when Sally Benson is waiting?* "Excuse me."

"So, you liking it?" he asked before she could turn away.

"What?"

"The life. LA. The whole scene."

She stood straight and smiled. "I was born for this."

"Cool . . . because to be honest I was a little surprised when I heard you signed with Sapphire."

She studied him closely now. What was he saying—was that meant as an insult? "Why?" she asked cautiously.

"Oh, nothing bad. Just . . . you and your dad . . . you played at our church a couple of years ago."

Grace tried not to act shocked. This guy had been in one of those churches? Why hadn't he told her that before?

"We were living in Florida, my family and I."

An unwanted flashback slapped her right across the face. A pathetic Grace, wearing a sad little hand-me-down dress, singing like a puppet, sitting like a mouse on the pew . . . so humiliating. "Uh, what was your name again?" she asked meekly.

"Quentin." He peered curiously at her. "So, yeah, I kinda assumed you'd still be doing that kind of thing. I mean, I think it rocks that you're here. Definitely need light in this industry."

Grace felt completely dumbfounded. It was like he'd thrown a bucket of ice water over her head.

"Hey, I don't want to keep you. Looked like you were in a hurry."

"Oh, yeah. Right." Still feeling stunned, she turned away.

"When you see your dad," he called out, "tell him we're fans. And not just for the music, you know? He's touched a lot of lives with his message too."

Grace went into the women's restroom feeling like she had just been blindsided. Going into the stall, she forced herself to take some deep breaths and steady herself. No big deal. So what if some intern knew more about her past than she'd have liked. It wasn't like it was some big secret. Sure, she didn't want guys like Jay Grayson to know all these details. But what difference did it make if Quentin what's-his-name knew?

Feeling a little calmer—and way more down to earth—Grace entered the conference room.

"Well, there she is," Mossy said.

"And about time," a slightly dowdy middle-aged woman said in a gruff voice. Grace did a double take. This woman was none other than Sally Benson.

"I'm sorry," Grace told them. "But nature was calling, you know?"

They laughed, and the atmosphere in the room lightened a bit.

"Wait'll you see these photos," Kendra said. "You look so hot. And you were absolutely right about that cocktail dress, Gracie. It's perfect."

Grace went over to where they were gathered around a laptop and was shocked to see the layout for an article that appeared to be about her and Jay Grayson. "Who took these pictures?" she asked Mossy. "I mean, I saw paparazzi outside." She pointed to a shot of them walking into the restaurant. "But this one in the lounge?" She shook her head. "I didn't see anyone with a camera."

"You know how cameras are these days," Mossy told her. "Everybody's got one on their phone or—"

"But we were the only ones in there . . . at first anyway." She frowned to see the shot of her holding her cocktail glass and laughing happily. What would her family and friends say when they saw that? Maybe it didn't matter. Maybe it was for the best. It was about time everyone figured it out. Gracie Trey was in it for the long run. Gracie Trey was here to stay. Before long she was seated across from Sally and, with the mic in front of her, she was answering questions for Sally's blog.

"So tell me, Gracie," Sally said, "how did you meet Jay Grayson."

"Jay came to one of my shows. Mossy introduced us, and we just hit it off. He's a really fun guy."

"Is he a good kisser?" Sally asked with arched brows.

"Oh, we've only had one date," Grace said quickly.

Sally gave her a doubtful look.

"Can I inject something," Kendra said. "To help Gracie. Didn't you say you'd edit this later?"

"Sure," Sally said eagerly. "Gracie could use some help. Otherwise we'll be putting my fans to sleep with this."

"How about if Gracie returns it with a question?" Kendra pointed at Grace. "Sally asks you 'Is he a good kisser?' and you say, *'What do you think, Sally?'* and put a little sass in it, okay?"

"I like it," Sally confirmed.

Grace gave Kendra a look now—like what? But Kendra just returned with a *trust-me* look. Just then Mossy's assistant stepped into the room. She whispered something to Mossy, and he nodded. "Send him in," he said quietly.

"We'll step away from Jay for the moment," Sally told Grace. "Let's talk about your dad instead. He gave up his career for religion. What's he doing these days?"

"He's a full-time music pastor at our—I mean—*his* church."

"I get it." She wrote something down in her notebook. "I assume he brought you up religious. How has that affected you as an artist?"

Grace was just trying to think of a good answer when there was another knock at the door. Mossy opened it, and this time Quentin was there. In his hands was a vase full of red roses.

"Come in," Mossy said warmly, as if expecting him.

"Thanks. These are for Grace. And they're, uh, not from me."

She tossed him an awkward smile. Did he really think she'd assume he'd brought her roses?

"Sorry for the interruption," Quentin stepped back to the door.

"Hey, stick around," Kendra called to him. "In case Gracie needs something."

Looking a little uneasy, Quentin remained by the door, watching as Grace removed the card.

"So, who's the secret admirer?" Sally asked in teasing tone.

Grace read the card. "They're from Jay," she said quietly.

Sally slapped the table. "Sure they are. Of course. This is priceless. Readers will love it. Jay Grayson sends . . ." She peered at the bouquet. "Not just one dozen, mind you, but two dozen perfect red roses." She chuckled. "That's fantastic. Just perfect."

Kendra moved the roses to the other end of the table, and Sally turned back to Grace. "All right, where'd we leave off?" She looked back at her notes. "Oh, yes, your dad's religion. How's that affected you, Gracie?"

Grace hadn't meant to make eye contact with Quentin, but it was too late. He returned her gaze with the tiniest of nods, as if to encourage her . . . but to do what?

"Well, my dad, he um . . ." She tried to form her words. "Well he takes his faith very seriously. He . . . he's all about God, and . . . stuff. But he's just really happy for me and excited that I'm doing this."

Mossy smiled at her, as if this was just what he wanted her to say, but Quentin looked slightly confused.

"Is that good enough?" Grace asked Sally.

"It's your interview," Sally said in a flat tone.

Grace could tell by Kendra's expression, she was flunking this test. "This is all so new to me," she confessed. "I know it should be more interesting. I just don't know how . . ."

Kendra sat down next to her now. "Look, Sally," she said gently. "This girl needs a little coaching. Mind if I help out some more?"

"Not at all." Sally made a tired sigh. "Someone needs to pump some life into it."

So now, with Kendra at her side, and with Grace's eyes fixed on the bouquet of roses, not Quentin, they tried it again. This time Grace made an effort to be more engaging and interesting and, thanks to Kendra's quick wit and support, she made it through the interview with what Mossy said were "flying colors." Unfortunately, she knew that some of the colors she'd flown with were shading the truth a bit. But, really, she gave them what they wanted, didn't she? Who could fault her with that?

# Chapter 15

**G**etting ready for her second date with Jay, Grace felt much more relaxed. As before, he picked her up at her apartment, but this time he just called her from down on the street. "I don't really like to leave my car out here." He explained. "Not that I don't like your neighborhood, but I do like my car."

"No problem," she told him. However, as she went down the stairs, she couldn't help but feel slighted. Did he like his car more than he liked her? Yet, when she saw his brilliant smile and as he opened the door for her, pausing to compliment her dress, all reservations about Prince Charming vanished.

"Thanks for the roses," she told him as he drove off fast. "They're absolutely beautiful."

He gave her a slightly bewildered look but quickly recovered. "American beauties for an American beauty."

She stretched her arms out, catching the warm night air in her hands. "What a gorgeous evening!"

"A great end to a great week," he added. Once again Jay gave her the lowdown of his workday. Fortunately, it seemed to have been a better one than his day on their last date. In fact, he seemed to be flying high.

They went to the same restaurant as before, and the same two valets met them, treating them like royalty, and this time they even knew who Grace was. Naturally, that made her walk tall as they went inside. She could so get used to this. Once again they were ushered off into the private lounge, and Jay simply motioned the waiter, and it seemed like less than a minute before two drinks were placed in front of them. A Cîroc-tini with three olives for her and a Black Bull for Jay.

"That's what I call service, Bobby." Jay winked at him as he lifted his drink to Grace. "Here's to another great evening with the most beautiful girl in Hollywood."

She felt her cheeks warm as she lifted her drink. And, as she took a sip, she tried not to think about the photos that were posted on Sally Benson's blog right now or the caption insinuating that Gracie Trey was turning into a party girl. One little martini with your date did not mean you were ready for celebrity rehab. It was simply a fun way to wind down after a week of hard work. And she had worked hard this week. Between publicity appearances at radio stations and another show last night, she needed a break. Besides that, she was supposed to be working on her new song, but she did not want to think about that tonight.

As a result, when Jay waved to Bobby for another round, she didn't even protest. Why not? She'd worked hard; she deserved to have some fun. She gazed into his handsome face and sighed. "How does it feel to be at the top of your game?" she asked him with what she knew was bordering on adoration.

He beamed back at her. "Well, I'm not sure I'm at the top of my game just yet."

"But you're one of the hottest TV stars, Jay. Everyone knows who you are."

He nodded. "That's true. But maybe I want more than TV."

"Movies?"

He shrugged. "Sure, why not."

"You'd be totally awesome up there on the big screen, Jay. Really, you would." She could feel her head swirling a bit but didn't want him to know. "I would gladly buy a theater ticket to watch you."

He laughed. "You, my darling, would not have to buy a ticket."

She laughed too. "Well, thank you—thank you very much."

"Elvis fan?" he teased.

Suddenly she realized she'd actually been imitating her dad, imitating Elvis, but she simply nodded. "Yeah." She held up her nearly empty martini glass. "Here's to the king of rock and roll."

He held up his glass. "And here's to the new queen of rock and roll—Miss Gracie Trey."

Now she felt slightly worried. "Oh, Jay, do you really think I'll ever make it that big?" she asked.

"Sure you will. You're already on your way. A hit single. A video coming out soon. And Sapphire begging you for an album."

She frowned as she took a sip. Had she actually said that? That Sapphire was *begging*? Sure, they were asking her for her next song . . . but begging? No, she didn't think so.

"But I *have* to make it," she said urgently. "I mean I just *have* to. . . . I can't go back." For some unexplainable reason— unless it was the booze and an empty stomach—she felt very close to tears now. Or like she was in the midst of climbing a tall mountain but couldn't get beyond halfway to the top.

"You will make it, Gracie. You're a star. Everyone can see it."

"You really think so?" She looked hopefully at him.

"No question." He nodded to her empty glass. "Let me get you a fresh one."

"Oh, I shouldn't."

"No, it's cool." He waved to Bobby, holding up two fingers for the next round. Then he looked back at Grace with an intensity that caught her off guard. And suddenly she felt the need to fill the air with conversation.

"You know what's scary," she said quietly, "is they've still only signed me to the single."

He looked surprised. "I didn't know that."

"Yeah, and if it doesn't *trend*, then, well, who knows."

"But it's on the radio all the time. Must be doing good." Bobby set the next round in front of them, removing the empty glasses.

"It started off so great. But now my manager tells me the downloads are flat." She picked up the fresh martini and held it up, peering at the wavy looking liquid and three green olives. "Flat. Flat. Flat." She shook her head. "That's all he says."

"Really?" Jay's brow creased with concern.

"Yeah, he tells me not to worry, but . . ." She rolled her eyes dramatically. "Oh, yeah, and then there's my follow-up song." She let out a loud groan.

"What's wrong with it?"

She leaned forward now, like she was telling him a huge secret. "Okay, now you can't tell *anyone* this. But I'm s'posed to write this follow-up song, you know, if 'Misunderstood' does good enough and everything. 'Cause I told them I was a writer. . . ." She waved a warning finger in front of his face, but it was all starting to look a little blurry. "But—and I'm serious—you can't tell anyone. . . . *I lied.*" She grimly shook her head. "I *never* wrote a song in my life. Not a good one anyway." Now she threw back her head and laughed like this was the funniest thing in the world. Jay laughed too.

"And it's not like I don't try," she told him with slurred-sounding words. "I do. I try my hardest. Problem is I jus' can't do it."

"Just do another one of you dad's songs," he suggested. "It'll be like your own thing."

"No!" She shook her head so hard that she saw two Jays instead of one. "That's the *last* thing I want."

"Why? What's wrong with your dad?"

She just laughed. "What's not wrong with him?" She held up a finger. "First of all, he *hates* what I'm doing."

"Get out."

"Well, not what I'm doing. But *how* I'm doing it . . . and everything." She took another sip and felt the tears coming again. Why was she being such a baby about this?

"What do you mean by *everything*?" he asked with what seemed like concerned eyes, like maybe he was the only one on the whole planet who really cared for her.

"I mean . . . I get that he just wants the best for me and everything. . . . But it's my life, you know?"

"Uh-huh."

"It's like his baby girl's not a baby anymore."

Jay nodded eagerly. "That's for sure."

"But in his mind I turned on him . . . and God . . . and everything. But I didn't really . . . you know? It's just that, well, maybe I was just never that into the God thing. Not as much as Dad thought I was." She looked at him with tear-filled eyes, trying to explain her feelings, her inadequacies where her father is concerned. She wondered if Jay really understood the depth of what she was saying. "You know?"

He looked slightly unsure, and she knew she was making him uncomfortable with her emotional display. What was wrong with her? "I'm sorry," she said as she used a cocktail napkin to blot her tears. "I don' know wha's wrong with me. I pro'bly said too much."

Jay reached across the table and stroked her bare arm. Gently he moved his hand up and down, nodding as if he really did understand. "It's all good," he assured her. "All good, you know? You can tell me anything. It's okay, Gracie." He set some money on the table, then reached for her hand. "Hey, listen, let's get out of here. Too many eyes watching us."

"Oh, yeah." She stood slowly, surprised that her legs felt slightly rubbery.

With his arm linked securely in hers, he was leading her out now. "Let's head to my place. You can tell me more about it there. Without anyone listening in on us."

She nodded, thinking that was a good idea. The last thing she needed was to read about this in Sally's next blog. But after they were in the car, driving with the top down and the fresh air on her face, she realized that going home with Jay was not such a good idea. Especially considering how lightheaded she was feeling. How many martinis had she had? And what had happened to dinner?

"Uh, Jay," she began uneasily as he stopped at a red light. "I, uh, I don't think I should go to your place after all."

"Why not?" He peered curiously at her. "The night's still young." He reached over and put his hand on her knee. "And I know you need to talk, baby. And I'm a good listener."

She nodded. "I know. But I shouldn't. I have to get up early . . . and . . . I'm not feeling too good, you know? I should probably just go home."

The light changed, and he removed his hand from her knee, gunning the engine and driving too fast through the intersection. He didn't say a word as he drove her back to her apartment. She didn't even remember going up the stairs or getting into bed. But the next morning, she woke up in her own bed . . . alone.

Grace sat up in bed, listening to what sounded like a knock at the door, but what really got her attention was the pounding in her head. Now she heard a jingle of keys, and Kendra was calling out to her. Grace flopped back onto her pillow, holding her head with her hands in an attempt to stop the pounding.

"Hey, Sleeping Beauty." Kendra came into her bedroom.

Grace forced herself to sit up again, still holding onto both sides of her head. "What time is it?" she asked.

"Ten o'clock. Must've been a fun night. But I am determined to finish today. So out of bed, sleepyhead."

Grace groaned as she shoved her feet out of bed and planted them onto the floor. "Oh . . ." She moaned, putting a hand back to her forehead.

"Looks like someone had a little too much fun." Kendra peered at her. "Having a little hangover, are we?"

Grace frowned. "Don't know about you, but I've had better mornings."

Kendra pointed toward the bathroom. "You get into the shower, and I'll get something to help you."

Grace shuffled toward the bathroom, but each step felt like someone had tied weights to her ankles. Eventually the water was pouring over her throbbing head, and it helped a little, but she still felt lousy when she got out. Why did people drink so much that they felt sick the next day? Why had she?

"Here you go," Kendra handed a bottle of water and an aspirin through the bathroom door. "Drink the whole thing. You're probably dehydrated. That's what gives you a headache."

Grace did as she was told. Then with her hair wrapped in a towel and wearing her terry robe, she came out to where Kendra was laying out some clothes. "Go get yourself some juice," Kendra said. "Get your blood sugar up."

"Okay," Grace muttered as she continued on into the kitchen. She wanted to ask how Kendra knew so much about this stuff—except she already knew the answer—personal experience. Grace poured herself some cranberry juice and slowly sipped it and returned to the living room to stand like a mannequin while Kendra held up various items of clothing to Grace—the paper doll routine again. Then Kendra would lay the garments out on the couch, layer on accessories and belts and shoes or boots, building a wardrobe with more than enough outfits to choose from.

Next Kendra had Grace try some of the clothes on to make sure the fit was right. Then she made lots of notes in her notebook, mapping it all out so that the shoot would go as smoothly as possible. After about an hour Grace started feeling better. Not like her usual self but well enough to cooperate with Kendra as she picked the final outfits for the video shoot. These were the clothes Grace would eventually wear when the cameras were rolling. Thankfully they were not rolling this morning.

"Time for coffee," Kendra announced. "You do have a coffeemaker don't you?"

Grace nodded.

"Coffee and dry toast," Kendra explained as they went into the kitchen. "Part three of my personal remedy for hangovers."

"Okay, Grace started making coffee while Kendra made some toast.

"And some more juice won't hurt either," Kendra told her.

By the time Grace finished Kendra's "remedy," she actually did feel better. Not great by any means but definitely better. She thanked Kendra. "I don't know what I'd do without you," she told her, watching as Kendra made some more notes.

"Most of the time I feel pretty lost anyway. But it's reassuring to know that you're watching my back."

Kendra held up a short, flouncy skirt to Grace's waist, eying it carefully then shaking her head no. "Yeah, I watch your back and your front and every other angle," she joked. "Gotta keep our superstar looking hot."

Grace slumped down into a chair. "I sure don't feel like a superstar today."

"Hey, everyone overimbibes sometimes, Gracie. Don't beat yourself up."

"That's not it," Grace said dejectedly. "I mean, yeah, I'm not proud that I got drunk. But I was talking more about my music. I sure don't feel like a superstar when Mossy tells me my sales have gone flat."

"Everybody's sales go flat at times. But when they're as talented as you are, they pick up again. Besides that's what the video's for—to give a boost to the single. And then there's your next song. It'll boost things too. Trust me, Sapphire knows its business. So does Mossy. Sales might be flat for awhile, but we're all working to change that."

"But what if it *doesn't* work? What if this ride is about to end?" Grace felt teary-eyed again. "I don't know what I'll do if I fail."

"Stop worrying about it. And don't forget that we're still in the top fifty, Gracie. Really, you're doing fine."

Grace still felt unsure, and the idea of her crawling back home was truly disturbing. To have to admit to her parents that they were right and she was wrong . . . well, it was too hard to think about. Kendra held up a vest then looked directly into Grace's eyes.

"Baby," Kendra said gently, "the media hits are just starting. We'll get a bump. I promise you. Just give it time." She tried a scarf now, looping it around Grace's neck a couple of times. "And WideSpin alone has eighteen million uniques. Eighteen million!"

Grace brightened. "That's a lot."

"You bet that's a lot." She held up some big hoop earrings. "Plus, people need to see you. Seriously, when they see you, they'll *buy* you. Which is why we need you to look hot for the video, and we want you to look hot for a certain actor." She winked as she tried some dangly beaded earrings. "It will all work out, Gracie. I believe in you."

Grace relaxed a little. She wanted to believe Kendra. "Hey, that looks good," she pointed to the last outfit Kendra had assembled. "I like it."

"I do too." Kendra nodded with satisfaction as she started to box up the ensembles into separate boxes. Everything was marked and numbered, and Grace knew that with Kendra in charge of her appearance, she was in good hands. "There." She dropped her pen and tablet back into her bag. "Now, we'll just leave the boxes here for the intern to pick up, and he can bring them to the shoot."

"Okay," Grace frowned. "Except don't give him a key this time."

"Why? Is he hitting on you? I'll fire him."

"No, no, I just . . . you know, I don't like him having a key to my place. Actually why does anyone besides me have a key?"

"It's standard, baby." Kendra reached for another box—not one of the ones that contained the video outfits—this one was shiny and pink and mysterious looking.

"What's that?"

Kendra made a sly grin. "Got you a present. Go ahead, open it."

"Seriously? *For me?*" Grace untied the ribbon.

"Yeah, I was doing some shopping for myself, and I saw this and thought it would be perfect for you." She giggled as Grace extracted something red and lacy from the tissue paper. "Or maybe it's more for Jay."

Grace studied the skimpy lingerie. She'd never owned anything like this in her life . . . never wanted to. In fact, she and Rachel used to make fun of garments like these, laughing over why any girl would lower herself to wear something so skanky, not to mention uncomfortable.

"Oh, my," Grace felt her cheeks warming with embarrassment. She didn't know what to say. "Uh, thanks."

"Isn't it great?" Kendra exclaimed. "Jay's gonna love it. Or you in it anyway."

"You really think he's *that* kind of guy?" Grace asked quietly.

Kendra looked at Grace as if she'd just sprouted a second head. "Baby," she said slowly, "every guy's that kind of guy."

Grace placed the sleazy piece back in the box, covered it with pink tissue, and securely replaced the lid. Then, forcing a smile at Kendra, she tried to sound grateful as she thanked her again. But she could sense Kendra looking at her now, studying her closely, almost as if she thought Grace had come here from another planet. And maybe it was true, maybe she had.

# Chapter 16

On Saturday night, Grace was scheduled to play at the Roxy. As always, she arrived early with her stylists; and after security let them in, they made their way backstage. Grace was surprised at how normal this was all starting to feel. Walking into a club or a theater and feeling like she belonged, like she was welcome. As she headed back to the dressing room with her entourage in tow, she thought how this felt just like a scene from a movie—only this was way better because it was her life.

Kendra had just gotten her all dressed, and Phoebe was putting the finishing touches on her hair and makeup when Mossy burst into the room.

"Hey, you ever hear of knocking?" Grace asked as she strapped on her guitar.

"I figured if you weren't ready to get out on stage, you deserved to be surprised."

"What's up?" she asked. She could tell by his face that something was going on.

"The WideSpin bump was bigger than expected," he told them.

"Really?"

"You just got the green light for the radio tour."

"No way!" Grace was dancing around the room, high-fiving Phoebe and Kendra.

"Congrats," Phoebe told her.

"Way to go," Kendra made a knowing nod. "See, I told you not to worry."

Grace grinned happily. "And you were right."

"But that's not all," Mossy said.

"What?" Grace demanded. "Hurry and tell me before I have to go out."

"Sapphire wants to contract the follow-up song!" he exclaimed.

"That's awesome," Phoebe said.

"Cause for celebration." Kendra held up her glass.

"Wow," Grace didn't know what to say. She knew she should be wildly excited, but all she felt was anxiety.

"And . . ." Mossy gave her a sly look.

"And?" She studied him. "There's more?"

"They want to record before you leave on the radio tour."

"Before the tour?" She tried to act enthused.

"Gotta keep the machinery rolling," he said. "They'll be getting it ready to release while you're touring. When it comes out, it'll give a fresh boost to the single. And then the single will boost the new song." He laughed. "And that's just the beginning!"

"Gracie Trey," the stage manager yelled into the dressing room. "You're on in five."

"Knock 'em dead," Phoebe told her.

"Rock the house," Kendra added.

*"Gracie Trey is here to stay!"* Moss called out.

Johnny looked at the digital clock on the kitchen stove as he poured himself a glass of milk. "It's three-thirty AM," he said aloud. "Do you know where your child is?" He took a swig and sadly shook his head. Then, feeling hopeless and depressed, he went out to the living room couch, where he'd been camping on other sleepless nights like tonight. He didn't know if the milk actually helped, but he preferred it to the Tylenol PM pills he'd tried last week. They left him feeling too fuzzy and sleepy in the morning.

He considered turning on his computer but knew where that would get him. He'd start out by doing a Google search of Grace's name—aka *Gracie* Trey. That would bring all sorts of disturbing things to the surface, including a gossipy music blog where photos of his little girl drinking and partying with Jay Grayson would pop up. Or else he'd start to write her an e-mail, attempting to pour out his heart and beg her to come home. But it would get longer and longer until even he could see how pathetic it sounded. And he knew she would hate it. So he would delete the post and start cruising the net and end up reading frightening stories about unfortunate singers or actors who'd made bad choices or simply been the victim of someone else's bad choice.

He couldn't take much more of that. And so he would just sit there in the darkness, attempting to pray, but most of the time he ended up berating himself for allowing this to happen. Because, despite what Pastor Tim and Michelle kept telling him, he did blame himself. He wasn't absolutely sure what he could've or should've done differently. But as the head of this household, as Grace's father, he knew it was his job to protect. But how was he supposed to protect someone who refused his protection?

Finally, in his tired and depressed state, one particular word would assault him like a final blow. *Failure.* Johnny Trey was a failure. A great big failure. He had let everyone down.

"Can't sleep again?"

He looked up to see Michelle standing in her nightgown with the hallway light behind her. He couldn't make out her face in this light, but he knew her expression—a mixture of sleepy concern and disappointment.

"I'm all right," he grumbled. He wanted to tell her to just go back to bed, but he knew where that would get him. A fight.

"I know you can't sleep, but why don't you at least come back to bed?"

Now he wanted to tell her to just leave him alone. What difference did it make to her if he was awake out here or awake in bed? He was *awake*. Get over it. But he knew that would only hurt her feelings. And even though he felt angry, he didn't want to hurt her . . . not anymore than she was already hurting.

"Fine," he said in a gruff voice, pushing himself from the couch to his feet.

Michelle folded her arms across her front, letting out an exasperated sigh. "Forget it," she snapped as she turned and walked back to the bedroom.

He just stood there watching as the hall light went off, listening to the solid sound of the bedroom door closing. Perhaps she'd even locked it. Not that he cared. Not that it even mattered. It was as if their missing daughter was turning into a giant wedge that was getting pounded, one day at a time, between them. Oh, sure, they both knew how to pretend they were okay. They knew how to give the right answers. But as time wore on, they were not getting better. Not really.

Michelle gave Johnny plenty of space as they got ready for church the next morning. He could tell she was trying to stay out of his way, as if she was worried that she might rub him wrong. Naturally, this only made him feel worse. He already felt guilty for pushing her away last night—yet he wasn't even sure how to apologize to her. If he said he was sorry, that he'd wanted to be alone, it would hurt her feelings, and they would be right back where they'd been last night.

He forced a smile as he came into the kitchen. "Smells good," he said as he poured coffee. "Been baking?"

"Blueberry muffins," she said in a slightly robotic voice.

"Mmm . . ." His smile grew more genuine.

"You can have one if you want, but they're really for the Bryants."

"You're taking them to church?"

Her brow creased as she handed him a plate with scrambled eggs and sausage on it. "Did you forget that you invited them over here for lunch after church?"

"Oh, yeah." He nodded as he sneaked a muffin from the basket by the stove.

Johnny sat down at the breakfast nook, then looked over to where Michelle was still fussing around in the kitchen. "You aren't joining me?"

"I already ate," she said over her shoulder. "I need to wash up these baking things and clean up the kitchen for lunch. I'm sure the Bryants will be right behind us when we get home after church. Don't want them to walk into a mess, do we?"

Johnny just shook his head as he reached for a napkin. No, they certainly wouldn't want the pastor and his wife walking into a mess, would they? As if their lives weren't in a complete and messy upheaval since Grace had run off. Really, who did she think they were fooling? Out of habit, he bowed his head, but besides a perfunctory blessing his heart didn't feel the least bit connected to God.

Neither of them spoke on the way to church. But Johnny welcomed the silence, hoping that it would give him a chance to get his spirit in a more worshipful place. However, as they walked into the sanctuary, he had his doubts. Today would be a day when God's strength would have to be made perfect in weakness. Because he felt whipped.

Somehow Johnny managed to lead the worship team. And, naturally, since Grace wasn't around, there were no slipups or surprises—everyone performed exactly as they'd done at rehearsal. Johnny should've been glad. But all he felt was empty as he went through the mechanics. It was as if some of the heart had gone out of his music, as if it had left with his daughter.

After the service, the Bryants followed them home as planned. As usual, Johnny and Michelle managed to put on their game faces as they welcomed the older couple into their home. As lunch was served, they both managed to act perfectly normal, as if this thing with their daughter wasn't tearing them apart. How much the pastoral couple could see through this act was anyone's guess. And sometimes Johnny didn't even care. But then he remembered his job, their livelihood. He worked for the church—Pastor Tim was his boss. How would it look if the worship minister was falling to pieces?

"We know this has been hard on you," Sharon said as the four of them had coffee in the living room. "And you two are always in our prayers. You know that."

"And Grace too," Tim added.

"If you ever need to talk," Sharon said gently, "you know that we're here for you."

"We'll be all right," Michelle assured them. "Really. It's just hard sometimes."

"Of course." Sharon nodded.

"I know Johnny still blames himself sometimes." Michelle shot him a cautious glance. "Deep down, you know that's not why she left, *don't you?*"

He tried not to feel irked that she'd said this in front of Tim and Sharon. But acting nonchalant, he simply shrugged.

"That's right." Tim nodded with a compassionate expression. "It's times like these when everything we've ever learned is put to the test and we have to decide if we're going to believe His word. Are we willing to live it out in our lives? To *walk the walk?*"

Johnny knew his answer should be 'yes.' He *wanted* it to be yes. But at the same time he still wanted to protect Grace too. Wasn't that what dads were supposed to do?

Tim looked from Johnny to Michelle. But then he turned back to Johnny and continued. "It's times like these when we have to think on what is true," he said gently. "Really meditate on it. We have a Savior who loves us. We have a Savior who gave His blood for us. And we can rest knowing, I mean, really *knowing* that His Word is true. He will work all things together for good for those who love Him. We may not see it now, but eventually God will be glorified through all this."

"I think it's only natural for you to feel somewhat responsible," Tim said to him. "That's what parents do. But you need to remember that Grace made her own choice. You realize that, don't you?"

"Maybe in the daylight." He looked intently at his pastor, his boss. Maybe Tim deserved the truth. "But sometimes in the middle of the night, well, there's too much time to think. Some nights are tough."

"That's true for everyone," Tim assured him. "Our fears are always the worst in the darkness of night. But you can't let this paralyze you, John. God still has more work for you."

"That's what I've been trying to tell him," Michelle said. "But sometimes he has a hard time hearing it from me."

"That's not so unusual." Sharon smiled at her husband. "Sometimes we wives are the last ones our husbands listen to.

Sometimes all we can do is keep loving them and keep walking by faith."

"Maybe, but it wasn't always like that with Johnny and me." Michelle looked longingly at Johnny. "You *used* to listen to me," she reminded him. "We used to be a team. Now it feels like you're shutting me out."

"That's because you don't live inside my head, Michelle." He tightened his grip on his coffee mug. He wanted to hold it together, and at the same time he wanted to be honest and transparent. "I know firsthand what happens to people in the music world," he told her. "I know what's out there, what Grace could get into. Maybe she already has. . . . I don't know. And sometimes I feel so . . . well, helpless." He looked down at his lap now. "No man likes to feel helpless."

"Look, John," Tim spoke with authority. "God may not be using you in Grace's life right now. In fact, he may never use you in her life again. But that's not always for us to understand. Our job is to be faithful to God. And at some point, when our kids grow up, we have to step back and just trust Him with our babies."

Johnny looked up at him, trying to force a smile. "Yeah, I get that." Did he? Did he really? Or was he just trying to sweep this all under the rug? "And I'll try to keep that in mind in the middle of the night."

"Me too," Michelle said quietly. "The truth is, I haven't been doing too well with trusting God when it comes to my daughter. But instead of thinking about how much I miss her, I will try to trust that God is watching out for her."

"You won't be sorry," Sharon assured her. "We can never trust God too much."

Tim nodded. "That's right. You will never go wrong trusting God. Never."

They visited awhile longer, and Johnny tried to convince himself that he was taking their advice to heart. He tried to believe that God would watch out for his child. He wanted to believe it. But the underlying feeling—the fear he could not shake—was that Grace was going to get hurt. *Badly hurt.* And if there was anything he could do to stop it, to prevent it, nothing and no one would be able keep him from running to her aid.

# Chapter 17

As she sat at her small dining table, Grace was determined. She was going to write a song if it killed her. But the harder she tried, the more it all seemed to elude her. Like a slippery bar of soap in a steamy shower, she tried to grab onto it, but the words and the lyrics and the notes just kept sliding away. Then just when she thought she had it in her grasp, she squeezed too tightly, and off it went flying.

She crumpled the page she'd just been working on and threw it to the pile growing on the kitchen floor. *Garbage.* It was just plain garbage. And to think anyone would want to listen to *that*, let alone pay money or even sample a free download, well, it was just plain ridiculous. "It's useless," she muttered as she leaned her tired head onto the table. "Hopeless." Why was she even trying?

Grace knew the truth, and it did not feel good. The truth was Gracie Trey was no better than Johnny Trey. In fact, she was not even as good. Sure, her dad might've been a one-hit wonder, but at least he'd written that one hit. All she'd done was rerecord it. She couldn't write a hit if her life depended on it. Gracie Trey was a complete fraud.

She stood up and started pacing. What was she going to do? What *could* she do? Finally, knowing that she had no answers, she simply stood and stared at the vase of red roses Jay had sent her. So elegant and sophisticated and completely out of place in her cheap little apartment. A cheap little apartment that she would not be able to afford once Sapphire Music discovered that she was a phony and incapable of producing a second song. She took a rose out of the vase and studied it. So perfect, so exquisite, so beautiful. American Beauties, Jay had told her. "For an American beauty." She smiled sadly as she slipped the rose back in with the others.

Now her eyes spied the shiny lingerie box sitting on one of the dining room chairs, right where she'd stashed it until she could decide what to do with it. For some reason it occurred to her that the risqué lingerie was almost exactly the same color as the roses. Curious to see, she opened the box and removed it, holding it next to the roses. Perfect match. Almost as if it was meant to be . . . as if she and Jay were meant for each other. But were they really? And was Kendra right about guys? Was this what they really liked? What they expected? Was this what Jay had been hoping for? And if so, was Grace even ready for it?

As she carried the skanky lingerie back into the living room, thinking she'd put it back in the box and forget about it, her mind was still on Jay. What was he doing right now? And why hadn't he called her since their last date?

Well, of course, she knew the answer. She'd gotten so wasted that she'd ruined everything. But wasn't that partly his fault? Even so, she felt badly. She couldn't even remember what she'd said when she'd asked him to take her home. However, she did remember the disappointment in his eyes. Jay Grayson was probably not used to rejection. Perhaps it was time for her to call him and straighten this out.

She absently dropped the lingerie onto a box on the couch and went straight for her phone. Pushing the number she'd assigned to speed dial for him, she waited, longing to hear his voice. Instead she got his voicemail. Now she had to figure out what she wanted to say.

"Hey, Jay," she said in what she hoped was an enticing tone, "it's Gracie. So I was just thinking about you . . . and the other night. And, hey, I don't even know what I said exactly. I was a little . . . well, you know. Anyway, give me a call when you get this, okay? And I, well, I guess I'll see you when I see you. Bye."

As soon as she hung up, she wished she hadn't done that. So lame. So middle school. And she knew she sounded desperate . . . pathetic. If only there was a way to undo a message after it was sent. She was about to call him again, ready to leave him another message. She would say, "Hey, forget that first message and have a great day!" But before she could hit speed dial, there was a knock at the door.

Could it be him? She fluffed her hair and poised herself, ready to act sophisticated and nonchalant. He didn't need to know how silly she'd just been. "Coming," she called cheerfully and, without even checking the peephole, she swung the door wide open and was taken aback to see that instead of Jay it was Quentin.

"Oh." She frowned at him.

"Not who you were expecting?" he said cautiously.

"No, I mean, no I wasn't expecting anyone."

"Uh-huh." He nodded but looked unconvinced.

She tried to act natural, but something about him standing there, studying her, it was almost like he could see right through her. And she did not need anyone—especially this obnoxious intern—to start judging her.

"Anyway, sorry to bug you," he said. "I'm here to pick up the clothes for the shoot. Kendra asked me to come—"

"Oh, yeah." She stepped out of the way. "They're over there."

Now Quentin held out a Ziploc bag of cookies toward her, making what seemed an embarrassed smile. "These are, uh, from my mom." He grimaced like this was uncomfortable. "Chocolate chip. Homemade. Mom, well, both my parents, remember you pretty well. You know from that night at our church in Florida."

Grace took the bag of cookies, wondering, *Who were these people?* But she tried to act natural. "Oh, cool." She forced an awkward smile. "Thanks. Tell your mom thanks."

"No problem." He went over to the couch now, stacking up the boxes.

Not wanting to stand there staring at him, she took the cookies to the kitchen, then sat back down at the dining table. She picked up her notebook, pretending to be studying some of the few lines that seemed to have potential, and acting like she was in the midst of some serious songwriting, waiting for him to gather up the stuff and just leave.

"So, what are you up to?" he asked as he set a stack of boxes by the door.

"Oh, just working on my new song," she said lightly.

"Cool." He returned to the couch. "How's it coming?"

She looked up, trying to think of an answer that wouldn't make her feel like too much of a liar and a hypocrite since for some reason it seemed like this guy knew the difference. But instead of answering honestly, she simply said, "Good." And that's when she saw it—Quentin was reaching for the box where she'd tossed the red lacy lingerie. Without saying a word, he picked it up—like he thought the skanky underwear was going to be part of her video shoot.

She jumped up to retrieve them. "No, not these," she said quickly as she grabbed them up. "Kendra got them by mistake, so we . . . they're not going."

"Okay." He picked up the stack and took them over to the door.

Feeling awkward and self-conscious, she returned to the table, once again pretending to be focused on the important work of songwriting. *Hurry and go*, she thought. But he seemed intent on taking his time, even making small talk, as he first stacked the boxes beside the door, then leaving the door ajar, he slid them outside.

"Oh, hey," he said when it looked like he was about ready to leave. "I made a promise." He came over to the table looking a bit like a shy schoolboy. "And it's gonna sound totally crazy 'cause you don't even know us, but my mom . . . she wanted me to tell you that if you ever want a home-cooked meal, well, she'd love to have you over." He made a sheepish grin. "So there. I kept my promise."

"Oh, wow." She set her pencil down. "Tell your mom thanks . . . and for the cookies too."

"Yeah, I will." He smirked. "And don't worry, I already told her that you're a big star and that you'd never spend time with someone like her."

Grace frowned. "You said *that*?"

"No." He chuckled. "Kidding. But, anyway, no pressure. But I will tell you this, my mom makes a mean—" He stopped himself, shaking his head. "Never mind. . . . She's a horrible cook, but she's a nice lady. I'll see you at the shoot." He headed for the door.

"Yeah, see ya."

"And I'll be praying for your new song."

She thanked him again, waving as he closed the door. Then she jumped up and after she dead-bolted the door, she grabbed the skimpy red lingerie from the couch and tossed the embarrassing pieces back into the box, closing it up, and then she went and slid it under her bed. Out of sight, out of mind.

The big day had come, and Grace felt ready for it as she walked into the recording studio where they planned to shoot the music video. The film crew was already setting up with Mossy looking on. Introductions were made, then Mossy told her that Kendra and Phoebe were waiting for her in the dressing room. "It's gonna be a great shoot," he told her. "Full of surprises."

"Surprises?" She frowned at him.

He chuckled. "Good surprises."

"Oh. . . ." She nodded.

"Go get ready," he commanded. "Time is money right now."

"Yes sir." She hurried off to the dressing room where Kendra and Phoebe were ready to go.

"This is your first outfit." Kendra pointed to the rack, then returned to steaming the wrinkles out of a dress.

Before long Grace was dressed up and made up, with every hair in place.

"Perfect," Kendra proclaimed.

"You look hot," Phoebe concurred.

"It's fun having such a gorgeous girl to work with," Kendra said.

"Thanks." Grace smiled at them.

"Yeah, if this music thing doesn't work out for you, you might consider taking up modeling," Phoebe teased.

"Yeah, right, Phoebs." Kendra rolled her eyes. "Maybe you haven't heard her sing."

Phoebe laughed. "Yeah, yeah, the girl's got it all going for her. A triple-threat in the world of music—she sings and writes and is beautiful."

Grace forced a smile. *If only they knew.*

"Ready in there?" Mossy called from outside the door.

"I'm coming," she told him as she reached for her guitar.

"Let's rock this thing," Kendra said.

And soon Grace was rocking it. Lip-syncing to "Misunderstood" in front of the green screen, she danced and moved and air-played her guitar. Meanwhile the crew did their work, moving in and out for shots, running the fan to blow her hair, encouraging her that she was doing a fabulous job. And then it would be time for a quick wardrobe change, and they would do it all over again. She couldn't quite imagine what the footage would look like, but she knew once it was edited and put back together, it would be good. She trusted these guys. She could tell they knew their stuff.

Through the whole thing Mossy watched on approvingly, making suggestions occasionally but mostly just standing by the door with his arms folded across his chest. Quentin remained on hand too. At first it bugged her. But whenever anyone needed anything, Quentin was the one they sent running. And he never complained once.

Eventually Grace had gone through most of the outfits, and they'd done dozens of takes. She really thought they should be about finished. She knew she was getting tired of this. How many takes did they need for a few minutes of video?

Still, she didn't let her impatience show as she emerged in what seemed to be the last ensemble. Stepping into place, she listened as they directed her, rocking out to the sound of her own voice playing in the background. Then about midway through the song, someone walked into the studio, and the filming stopped.

"Didn't you see the 'Do not disturb. We're recording' sign?" a cameraman growled. Now everyone turned to see who'd interrupted their session, and Grace could not believe her eyes. Standing there, looking around the room with a slightly bored expression was *Renae Taylor.*

"Okay, cut," the director said. "Hey, Renae." He grinned at her.

"Don't stop for me," she told him.

"I think we got it," he told her.

Renae nodded toward Grace. "You're wonderful."

Grace steadied herself, trying not to look too starstruck. "And you're Renae Taylor."

"Everybody take ten," the director called out. "Meanwhile, we'll check out the footage and see if we've got enough to call it a wrap."

"Why don't you girls get better acquainted," Mossy suggested. He pointed to a door. "That conference room is free."

Soon they were seated at a long table, where Grace was trying not to gape at Renae Taylor. Was this for real? And, if so, how did it happen? What did it mean?

"I've been hearing a lot about you," Renae told her. "I love your song."

"Wow." Grace took a gulp from her water bottle. "I, um . . . you're a big reason I'm even out here. I'm a huge fan."

"That's very kind. You're probably wondering why I'm here." Renae picked up a pen from the table, twirling it around in her fingers.

"No, not really. I mean I'm just pumped meeting you. But he did mention, I mean my manger, he said you might stop by sometime . . . that you were thinking of me for your opening act—which would be amazing." She took another gulp of water.

"Well, I'm considering several girls." Renae seemed to be scrutinizing her now. Was she trying to decide if Grace measured up?

"Oh, yeah, totally." Grace tried not to act as uncomfortable as she felt.

"I try to get to know people before I think about traveling with them."

Grace nodded. "Yeah. I get that." She made a stiff smile.

"I read the WideSpin spread. Sally's so convincing it's hysterical."

Grace nodded again, trying to act like she knew what Renae meant, but feeling a little lost. "Yeah, she's . . . she's cool."

"I loved the bit about the flowers being delivered right during the interview. Seriously, whose idea was that?"

"The roses?" Grace was confused. "From Jay?"

Renae laughed. "Come on."

"They were from Jay Grayson," Grace clarified.

"You're funny, Gracie. And I like that." She made an amused nod. "Seriously, a guy like Jay Grayson wouldn't think to send flowers to his dying mom."

Grace shrugged, trying to play along, wanting Renae to like her. "Yeah, maybe not."

"So how long do they expect you to play house with him?"

Grace felt even more confused. What did Renae mean? Did she think they were living together? Still, she didn't want to show her ignorance—not to Renae Taylor. "They . . . uh, really didn't say."

She gave her a knowing look. "Well, you just have to beat them at their own game. And use them more than they use you. *All* of them. You'll get there. I can tell."

Grace really had no idea what Renae was saying—use who? Jay? Mossy? Her stylists? "Yeah," she murmured. "I appreciate the advice."

"And remember this, Gracie Trey," Renae glanced at her expensive watch, then stood. "Your body is the biggest asset you have. Tons of girls can sing. But very few of them have your good looks. It's your currency. Spend it freely." And just like that, Renae Taylor turned and left.

Feeling confused and bewildered and slightly disappointed, Grace just sat there trying to make sense of it. Renae wasn't anything like she'd expected. Oh, sure, she looked like Renae Taylor, superstar, but she had been so cool and aloof and jaded. Nothing like she came across on the stage or during interviews. It was almost like there were two completely different Renae Taylors.

But more concerning than that was how Grace got the distinct feeling that Renae did not like her. As if she didn't even *want* to like her. Renae certainly showed no interest in getting to know her better. In fact, it felt like Renae had already made up her mind about her. But then Grace wasn't sure. Maybe that was just how Renae was, playing her cards close to her chest. After all, Grace reminded herself, Renae couldn't have made it as far as she had in this business if she wasn't tough. And maybe that was what Renae was trying to tell Grace—be tough. Still, it made Grace sad. Renae Taylor in real life was nothing like Renae Taylor in concert. *Nothing.*

# Chapter 18

Grace wondered if it was considered a real date when the guy didn't come to your place to pick you up. Or maybe she was just hopelessly old-fashioned—not to mention inexperienced. Even so, she assured herself as she drove through Hollywood on her way to Jay's favorite restaurant, having her own wheels guaranteed her independence—she wouldn't have to beg Jay to take her home. Plus it gave her a legitimate excuse not to drink tonight.

She hadn't actually spoken to Jay. But, after he'd gotten her slightly desperate message yesterday, he called while she was shooting the video and left her a message. Then, by the time she returned his call that evening, she got his voicemail again too. Busy people with busy schedules . . . so Hollywood.

She pulled in front of the restaurant and waited as a parking valet, not two, slowly made his way to her car. Okay, she knew it wasn't an impressive car like Jay's, but what about customer service?

"Oh, Miss Trey," he said as she got out of the car. "I didn't know that was you."

She forced a smile as she handed him the keys. "That's okay."

"Jay's already here," he told her. "I mean . . . I assume you're meeting him." He looked uncomfortable, like he'd just stepped over some invisible line.

"Thanks." She held her head high and walked toward the door. As she went inside, she reminded herself that this was more than just a date—this was a mission. She'd been running Renae's strange words through her head—about Jay, the roses, Sally's blog. . . . It hadn't really made sense at the time, but today it seemed to fall into place. Renae was suggesting that Jay was not being completely honest with Grace. As she entered the private lounge, spotting Jay at his favorite table with his glass half full and his eyes on his phone, she was determined to get to the bottom of it.

She smiled confidently as she went over to join him. He wasn't the only one who knew how to act.

"My day just got brighter," he said, standing to kiss her on the cheek.

"Hey," she smiled as he pulled a chair out for her.

"So how's the video queen?" He sat across from her and smiled warmly.

"Great. How's the TV star?"

"Hungry."

She was slightly relieved that he was thinking of food instead of alcohol but at the same time suspicious. "You'll never guess who came by the shoot."

"Who's that?"

"Renae Taylor."

"Your hero." He nodded. "Cool. How's she doing?"

"Great. It was incredible meeting her. I'm still blown away. She's thinking about me opening for her."

"Right on!"

"Yeah, I mean she's looking at other people too, but . . ."

"You'd totally rock it."

"Yeah, it would be insane." Now she remembered her real mission. "You know, Renae said something else. It was kind of weird—"

Just then his phone rang, and he checked the number.

"Anyway," she continued awkwardly, "I can't stop thinking about—"

"Sorry." He held up his phone. "Gotta take this. My manager." He got up and walked away from the table, but as she watched him, she felt uncomfortably curious. She wasn't even sure why, but something about him did not feel right. She got even more suspicious as he went behind the wall near the restrooms.

Now she decided to pay a trip to the restroom herself, but instead of going around the corner and into the ladies room, she paused behind the partition, pretending she was answering her own phone. But really she was listening to the conversation just around the corner.

"I can't tonight," Jay was telling someone. "Yeah, I'm with her now." He chuckled. "She thinks I'm talking to my manager."

Her ears perked up even more as he paused. She wished she could hear who was on the other end.

"I already told you, man, her manger set it up. Scotty owed him a favor or something. He asked me to hook up with her for publicity shots, and I'm, like, whatever. And why not? I mean *she's hot*."

Grace felt her cheeks flushing—not from embarrassment but from anger. Still, she remained in place, acting like she was listening to her own phone.

"No, man. Not yet." Jay sounded pretty full of himself. "I was about to last time. But then she got all weepy about her dad, and I was like, whatever, no thanks." He laughed. "But no worries, I'll close. Tonight I'm sealing the deal."

Her anger was quickly boiling over to rage now, but she didn't move.

"All right, man," he said as if winding the conversation down. "I gotta bail. Call you after . . . with details. I might even send you a picture."

With the sound of his smug laughter echoing in her head, she made a dash for the exit, making it out before he returned to their table. Fighting back infuriated tears, she handed the valet her ticket, standing in the shadows while she waited for her car. Sure, she could've stuck around for the showdown. But what if she'd fallen apart on him? How humiliating would that be? Better to let him sit there and wonder.

As she drove home, she wasn't sure who she was more enraged at—Jay or Mossy. And to think she had trusted them both. How stupid and naïve could she be? Then as she went into her apartment, she wondered if Kendra wasn't involved in it as well. Those comments about what guys wanted—the skanky underwear, insinuations about Jay. And then there was Sally—according to Renae's insinuations, she was in on this too. Seriously, was there anyone in Hollywood she could trust?

As soon as she was in her apartment, she found the phone number of the apartment manager and called. "This is Gracie Trey." She tried to steady her voice. "In unit 207. I want my locks changed, please." When the woman asked why, she told her that she'd found her door open one day. "And it just makes me uneasy to think someone walked around in here. What if they come back?"

"Okay," the woman said. "I'll let my husband know."

"Thank you!" Grace hung up, then paced around the apartment, feeling like she wanted to break something or just scream. Finally she went over to the detestable roses and, grabbing them out of the vase, she carried them over to the trash can beneath the sink and crammed them into it. With tears streaming down her cheeks, she opened the refrigerator and pulled out the bottle of Cîroc vodka she kept on hand for Kendra, and mixing a generous martini, she took a small sip. And then she took a big one.

The next morning, after she used Kendra's remedy for hangovers, Grace put in a call to Mossy's office and, keeping her voice calm and even, asked if she could come in to talk to him.

"Sure, Gracie. I'll be in my office until one. Can you make it in by then?"

"Oh, yeah," she assured him. "I'll be there."

She cleaned herself up and dressed carefully, rehearsing what she planned to say, except that she never could get it quite right. Okay, she told herself as she got into her car, maybe she would have to wing it. Mostly she just planned to make herself heard.

As she passed through security and marched through the glitzy lobby and past the big screens and posters—some that were of her—she kept her eyes straight forward. As she rode up the elevator, her sense of betrayal seemed to rise with each floor number. And when she walked into Mossy's office, she was so full of righteous indignation that she felt like she was going to burst.

"We need to talk!" she declared.

He hopped up from his desk, closing the door behind her. "What's up?"

"*What's up?*" she demanded. "That's what I want to know."

"You sound upset." He pointed to a chair. "Want to sit down and discuss whatever it is calmly? Like grown-ups."

"Grown-ups?" she shouted. "Is that what you are? Because for a minute there I thought I was dealing with children—like middle school kids who play their stupid games, lying, cheating, betraying—"

"What are you talking about?" He sat down in his chair and, folding his hands on his desk, calmly gazed at her.

"I'm talking about you setting me up with Jay!"

He gave her a slightly exasperated look. "Is that all?"

"Is that all?"

"Look, it was a publicity stunt. Surely, you knew that it—"

"So you admit it! You did set it up. Even the flowers!"

"Who cares? Yeah, sure I did. But it's no secret that in this industry you gotta play—"

"This is not about *this industry*!" she yelled. "This is about me—*my life*! You set me up with Jay, and then he decides that his reward for returning somebody's favor for you is taking me to bed—"

"That wasn't part of the deal." He held up his hands with a nonchalant expression. "But, really, what did you expect?"

"What do you mean?"

"I mean, you liked him. He seemed to like you. What did you think—that he was going to put a ring on your finger?"

"No!" She glared at him. "I don't know what I expected, but not—"

"Well, I know what I expected." He slammed his fist on his desk. "Because of Jay I got WideSpin, and because of WideSpin, we got a *29 percent bump in downloads*! Not only that, but I got Renae Taylor's people thinking you should open for her! What more do you want?" He shook his head grimly, looking at her as if she was a spoiled brat throwing a hissy fit.

Even so, she was not going to let him derail her. "I want you to stay out of my personal life," she declared hotly.

*"Personal life?"* He leaned forward and glared at her. "Don't you get it? There is no more personal life! You have a radio tour coming up *and* a second single to record before you leave, which none of us have even heard!"

Grace slumped into the chair now. It felt like the foundation of anger she'd laid on the way over here had just been blasted out from under her.

"Look," Mossy said a bit more quietly, but with just as much firmness. "I'm sorry you're heartbroken over some pipe dream you were entertaining over Jay Grayson. That's the way things break. But now you have *one week* to deliver an original song. So maybe it's just as well that Jay baby is out of the way. Now you can focus on the real reason you're here."

*Focus. . . .* Grace thought numbly as she rode the elevator down. *Focus* on the real reason she was here—to play music, to write music, and to look hot. Wasn't that what everyone had been telling her? And for the most part she got it. She could play music, and thanks to her stylists, she could look hot. But when it came to writing that next song, she was hopeless. As she got into her car, she wished she'd just been honest about it. Why hadn't she just told Mossy the truth? In the heat of the conversation, she could've simply blurted it out, *I can't write a song to save my life, so fire me!*

Before she went home, she stopped by the grocery store. She told herself she was going in to get some fresh fruits and vegetables, but what she'd come home with was sugary cookies and salty chips, as well as a big bottle of vodka and another bottle of sweet vermouth. All thanks to the fake ID Kendra had provided weeks ago. As Grace unpacked her bag, she realized she'd forgotten the olives. Not that she needed them for what she had planned.

The next few days passed in a fuzzy, intoxicated blur. Each day started out the same, with her swearing to herself that she would put all her energy into writing a song and that she wouldn't touch a drop of alcohol. But by midafternoon the promise would be broken. A pile of wadded up pages of really bad lyrics would be littering the floor, and she would be hitting the bottle. Sometimes she didn't even bother to use a glass.

To say she hated herself would've been an understatement. Not only was she a crappy songwriter; she was on her way to becoming an alcoholic—and there didn't seem to be any way to stop it.

On Sunday morning she woke up with a throbbing headache and nausea that drove her to the bathroom where she emptied her stomach. Kneeling by the toilet, she used toilet paper to wipe off her mouth and the tears running down her cheeks. She felt gross and nasty and sick, and she hated herself for being so weak.

Longing for fresh air—or maybe just a fresh start—she shuffled over to the bedroom window and pulled back the drapes. She pushed open the window and inhaled the outside air. Sure, it was tinged with exhaust fumes and nothing like the fresh air back home, but it was better than her foul-smelling apartment, which had been closed up for days.

Feeling empty and spent and useless, she stared blankly down at the street. Church must've been over because the people, dressed neatly in their church clothes, were all congregating outside. They seemed to be visiting happily with one another, enjoying the sunshine, probably making plans for the day, having a good life. Meanwhile she was trapped up here in the prison of her own making.

# Chapter 19

One week after her confrontation with Mossy, she showed up at Sapphire Music to sing her new song—late. As she rode up the elevator, she felt waves of nausea washing over her—either the result of nerves, or the hangover remedy wasn't working. She steadied herself as she emerged from the elevator. Moving her guitar case to her other hand, she could feel her palms sweating. Wiping a palm onto her thigh, she realized that her jeans were stained—the same ones she'd been wearing when she'd passed out last night. She didn't even want to think what her hair and face looked like. If she wasn't so late, she would've stopped by the restroom to fix up a bit. If that was even possible.

But maybe it was better like this. Let them see Gracie Trey in all her glory, a burned-out rocker at her finest. And only eighteen too. She should make her father proud. As she walked into the big conference room, she decided she didn't care. Let them see her for what she was—a big fat liar.

"Sorry I'm late," she mumbled as she came into the room. Everyone there looked clean and tidy and buttoned up, as well as a bit impatient. But as soon as they got a look at her, their impatience seemed to transform itself into concern. They were probably worried about their bottom line—they'd invested their money into a failure. Well, they'd wanted her father's daughter, hadn't they? It seemed that she was delivering.

"Go ahead," Mossy told her with a furrowed brow. "Show us what you got, Gracie."

She opened her guitar case. Fumbling to extract her guitar and feeling like she'd never played before, she strapped it on and awkwardly made the adjustments. If she'd been standing up there in her underwear, she couldn't have felt more conspicuous.

"Okay then." She took in a breath. "Here goes." And trying to make it sound like she meant it, like she believed it was a good song, she started to play. But as she played, she could hear how weak it was. The lyrics were bad, and the tune was dull. It was entirely forgettable—if the listeners were lucky.

By the time she finished, she had hot tears running down her cheeks. "I'm sorry," she choked out as she dashed for the door. "I'm really, really sorry." As she was leaving the conference room, she heard Mossy speaking.

"I thought she could do it," he was saying.

Grace hurried down the hall. Ducking into the women's restroom, she entered the stall on the end and closed the door.

She wanted to die. And if it was possible to die from humiliation, she should be dead any moment. As she jerked off a length of toilet tissue to blow her nose, she imagined the headline—*Has-Been Rocker Gracie Trey Discovered Lifeless in Public Restroom.* She was just wiping her eyes when she heard the door to the restroom opening . . . footsteps. With her guitar still strapped over her shoulder, she quietly perched on the toilet, squatting like a baseball catcher so no one would guess she was in here. The last thing she needed was for a curious Sapphire employee to strike up a conversation with her.

"What was *that*?" It sounded like Phoebe's voice.

"I know. I've dropped pans in the kitchen that sounded better," Kendra said in a bitter tone. "Seriously, why did I waste my time on her? I mean I went beyond the call of duty with that girl. I thought she had what it took."

"She took us all for a ride."

"Well, at least Daddy wrote a song she could gravy train." Kendra's voice dripped with sarcasm.

"I know, right?"

Grace didn't think she could take anymore.

"I mean if she can't handle it, next contestant, please." Kendra laughed in a mean way.

"And if she thinks she can come in looking like something the cat dragged in and expect to win anyone over, she is—"

Grace jumped noisily down from the toilet and burst out of the stall with her guitar still strapped on. She locked eyes with a startled Kendra and gave her a long stone-cold stare before she turned to leave. But just as she reached the door, Kendra reached for her arm.

"*Gracie*," she exclaimed with worried eyes.

Grace just jerked her arm away and hurried on out. Then realizing that her guitar case was still in the conference room, Grace marched back down the hallway to get it. Thankfully the room appeared to be empty now. Except that when she got inside, there was Quentin cleaning up coffee cups and water bottles and pushing in chairs.

"Hey, how'd it go?" he asked cheerfully.

She glared at him as she grabbed up her guitar case. "Did you pray for my song?"

"Yeah," he said, looking at her with concern.

"*Well, it didn't work!*" She shoved her guitar into the case, snapped it closed, and stormed out of the room.

She was just past the women's restroom when Kendra came after her. "Gracie," she called, "just listen to—"

"Get away from me!" Grace hissed at her as she walked even faster.

"But Gracie—"

"Leave me alone!" She was just turning a corner when she felt someone grabbing her by the arm. In surprise, she turned to see Mossy.

"Come with me!" he commanded as he led her toward the elevators.

She knew it was useless to fight this. And besides, they might as well have it out here and now. The sooner he handed over her walking papers, the better off they'd all be. She'd had enough—she was fed up with all of them. She would prefer to be homeless and on the street than to keep jumping through Sapphire hoops. She could do what she'd seen other down-and-out musicians doing—sitting on a corner, playing guitar. People could throw coins into her open guitar case.

"Sit down," Mossy told her as they went into his office.

She sat down, watching him as he paced back and forth behind his desk.

"Why don't *you* sit down?" she said defiantly.

"Fine. I'll sit down," he huffed as he dropped into his chair. Now he shook his head. "I just don't get you. One week ago you came in here acting like I'm the devil and—"

"Yeah!" she shouted. "That's because you tricked me, Mossy. You lied about—"

"You're the one who lied, Gracie. You said you could write."

"I tried . . . but—"

"When I think how you stormed in here last week, accusing me of ruining your life, going on your little tirade. Then today—and look at you." He pointed at her. "I'd say you're doing a pretty good job of ruining your own life." He grimly shook his head as he looked through a pile of message memos, going through them like there was something more interesting than her in there, not that it would've surprised her. Probably the "next contestant."

She sighed, slumping down into the chair. "I'm sorry," she muttered.

"One hit and she falls apart," he said as if she wasn't even there. "Well, the apple sure doesn't fall far from the tree." He looked at her with what seemed like disgust but could've been something more. "Go on. Pull yourself together. I'll see what I can do to fix this."

Feeling like something smelly that her manager wanted to wipe from the bottom of his shoes, Grace picked up her guitar case and schlepped out of his office. On her way home she stopped by the grocery store to pick up a fresh supply of vodka. No vermouth this time. Just vodka.

By eight o'clock that evening, one of the vodka bottles looked dangerously close to empty. She held it up to the light, staring at it in fuzzy wonder. Had she really drank *that much?* And if she had, why was she still standing? She should be totally wasted by now. More than anything Grace wanted to pass out and flee the reality of the mess she had made of her short-lived career. She emptied the last of the vodka into the tumbler and went back out to the living room.

Disappointed that the booze wasn't providing the escape she longed for, she turned on her computer. She wasn't even sure what she was looking for—perhaps it was praise . . . or maybe condemnation, but she wound up at Sally Benson's blog on WideSpin. And today's headline threw her for a complete loop.

## Hard Drinking Renae Taylor Lashes Out in Public Tirade

Grace blinked and then read the stunning words again, repeating them slowly as she tried to absorb the meaning behind them. *Was it true?* Was the smooth and successful Renae Taylor really unraveling? Was it even possible? But, as if to substantiate this unfortunate news, several unflattering photos of an angry and intoxicated Renae Taylor were posted right along with it.

Grace slammed her laptop closed and, taking her drink with her, staggered across the room. Turning on the light by the front door, she caught a glimpse of a haggard-looking image in the mirror hanging there. With drink in hand, she leaned forward, peering at her reflection with a morbid curiosity—kind of like looking at nasty car wreck with fatalities. Was that really her? As horrid as the photos of Renae had been, Grace looked far worse. Greasy hair, pasty complexion, chapped lips . . . but the worst part of this picture was the empty, haunted eyes staring back at her. This ghastly image shook her so thoroughly that the glass of vodka slipped from her hand. Falling onto the tiled entry area with a loud crash, it shattered into shiny jagged pieces.

Shuddering, she turned away from the mirror and, leaning her back against the wall, she let out a low guttural groan as her knees buckled beneath her. Slowly sliding down the wall, she sank to the floor in a disgusting heap of hopelessness. Her career was ruined, her life was ruined. . . . Everything was ruined.

On the other side of the country, Johnny sat down at his computer and Googled his daughter's name. He'd been trying to control himself from this compulsion in recent days. After so many sleepless nights obsessively tracking Grace online, he knew it was futile. He'd waste hours trying to reassure himself that she was okay, but then he'd end up reading a horror story about some other young celebrity whose life had fallen apart. Naturally, that would send him down a whole different road of worry and fear and desperation. But thanks to his pastor's counsel, he'd controlled himself recently. As a result he'd had a few nights of relatively restful sleep.

But tonight he was simply curious. It wasn't the middle of the night; he didn't plan to obsess. He was only going to look . . . he wanted to see if she was still the bright rising star that the Hollywood gossips had been describing her as. Besides, Michelle hadn't gone to bed yet. She would make sure he didn't get carried away in his Internet search.

However, the first thing that popped up on the Google list was Grace's new video of "Misunderstood." Of course, he was curious. He downloaded it and watched with fascination as his daughter did a mesmerizing performance of the song he'd written so long ago. She was really fabulous. He played it again, this time put on his critiquing hat, ready to pick out any flaws or misses. But he could not find a single thing wrong with it. Grace was brilliant. Absolutely brilliant.

He could feel Michelle standing behind him now, looking over his shoulder at his computer screen as he played the video one more time. She was probably fretting that he was obsessing again. And who could blame her?

"You okay, Johnny?" she asked gently.

"Uh-huh." He studied Grace's expression as she finished the song. She seemed pleased with her performance too—as if she'd done a fabulous job and knew it. If he was ready to be perfectly honest with himself, he'd have to admit that it seemed like she was doing exactly what she was made to do. She was in her groove.

"So what're you doing?" Michelle asked with concern.

"Oh, Shel," he said in a slightly choked voice. "Grace is incredible, isn't she?"

Michelle came around to sit on the couch next to him. "Yeah, she is."

"No, I mean really," he insisted as if Michelle hadn't just agreed with him. "She is really phenomenal." He pointed to the computer. "Have you seen this video?"

She smiled and nodded. "Just a dozen or so times."

"But you never said anything?"

"I wasn't sure how you'd take it, Johnny. You know how you've been lately."

"Yeah, a basket case. I know." He closed his laptop and set it on the coffee table, looking into his wife's eyes. "Sorry."

"Hey, I'm sorry too. We've both been struggling through this thing. Is it possible that we're finally making a little progress?"

"I sure hope so."

He sighed to remember how great Grace had done on the video. "She just blew me away, Shel. I mean I always knew she was good. But she is way beyond just good."

"She had the best teacher," Michelle said softly. "In every way."

"You really think so?" He wasn't so sure. In so many ways it seemed like he'd been too hard on his talented daughter.

"She didn't learn to sing and play all by herself, Johnny. You gotta know that you had a lot to with it, don't you?"

"Yeah, I guess I helped her a little."

"A little?" Michelle frowned. "Johnny, you taught her everything she knows about music. You gave her the guitar and—"

"No doubt, some of it was learned. But a lot of it was already inside of her." He gazed up at a photo of Grace on the mantle. "There's no denying she's naturally gifted." He slowly shook his head. "God had a lot more to do with it than I did."

Michelle smiled at him. "I find your humility very attractive."

He grinned as he slipped his arm around her, pulling her close to him. "Come here."

She snuggled close to him, letting out what sounded like a relieved sigh, and for several minutes they just held onto each other in a way they hadn't done ever since Grace had left them.

"We're gonna make it," Michelle said quietly.

"Yeah, I think so. But not because of me."

"Because of God," she whispered.

Johnny sighed as he looked up at the ceiling. Then he took in a deep breath. Slowly releasing it, he could feel himself letting go. "Grace is Yours now," he prayed aloud. "All Yours." And he meant it.

# Chapter 20

The next day Grace woke up crumpled on the living room floor. She was in the same spot she'd collapsed into the night before. Only now she was fully aware, and her head was throbbing, her ears were ringing, and her mouth felt like someone had shoved a dirty sock into it. The morning sun was streaking through the apartment, illuminating her slovenly housekeeping as well as the shattered glass shards still littered in front of the door. Lovely.

She was just pushing herself to her feet, her Converse shoes crunching on the glass shards, when she heard someone knocking on her door. Who could it be, and how could she get them to go away? She peered through the peephole, then frowned. Quentin. Of course. Mr. Do Good.

"What do you want?" she growled through the door.

"You all right?"

"Yeah. I'm fine." She injected some lilt into her voice. "What's up?"

"That's what I want to find out. I hear that you've been a little out of pocket lately. I just wanted to make sure you're okay."

"I'm fine," she growled.

"You don't sound fine. And I know you're not returning your calls."

"I'll get back to them when I can," she said sharply.

"All right." There was a pause, and she wondered if he'd left; but peeking through the peephole, she saw him still standing in the hall with a troubled expression. "Can I get you anything?" he asked hopefully. "Maybe something to eat?"

Her irritation melded into sadness now. Such a sweet and conscientious guy. If he knew what a mess she was, he'd probably run fast in the opposite direction. "No, I'm good," she told him.

"Can I just come in and talk to you then? Just to make sure you're really okay."

Fighting her embarrassment over the state of her apartment, she slowly opened the door. "Come on in," she mumbled, stepping through the glass shards. "Welcome to the nut hatch."

He glanced around, then looked directly at her. "Have you been sick?"

"Something like that."

"When was the last time you ate?" he asked with concern. She shrugged.

"Well, you look like you could use a good meal. How about a cheeseburger?"

She grimaced. "No, thanks."

"A taco?"

She shook her head.

"Let's see what you've got in your fridge." He headed for the kitchen, slowly telling her what her options were and finally emerging with a small carton of yogurt and the partially consumed baggie of cookies. "Come sit down," he said as he led her to the dining table. "You eat and I'll clean up this mess."

As she sat there slowly eating the yogurt and nibbling on a cookie, Quentin got out the broom and dustpan. She watched as he carefully swept up the shards and took them to the kitchen. He picked up a few other things, then eventually came over to check on her. "Feeling better?"

"I guess," she mumbled without looking up. It was humiliating to be seen like this—so needy and pathetic and lost.

"So you think you can make it over to Sapphire today?" he asked. "I know they want to talk to you."

"Yeah, yeah," she said in a grouchy tone. "I'll be there."

"Okay. I'll see you later then."

As he let himself out, Grace stared at the baggie of half-eaten cookies Quentin's mother had been so kind to send to her, and Quentin was only trying to help. Why was she acting like such a troll? Tossing down her spoon, she sprang for the door and dashed down the corridor, calling out to Quentin. "*Wait!*"

He turned to look at her. "Yeah?"

A neighbor peered curiously as Grace went past him. And she knew she must look hideous, but she didn't care. All she wanted was to catch Quentin.

"What's wrong?" he asked with concerned eyes.

"I forgot to say *thank you*." She paused, catching her breath. "And I wanted to know. Is your mom's cooking really that bad?"

He made a funny expression. "You just ate some of the cookies, right?"

She made a wobbly smile, trying not to break into tears. "Yeah, I kind of liked 'em."

He smiled with compassion, almost as if he understood her better than she'd imagined. Maybe better than she understood herself. "So you'll come for dinner then?" he asked hopefully.

She nodded shyly.

"Cool. Tonight okay?"

"Sure." She stepped back, suddenly feeling uncertain.

"See you at Sapphire," he called cheerfully as she turned to hurry back to her trashed apartment. As she closed the door, she questioned herself—Why had she just done that? Simply because she was down and out and feeling lost? Did she really expect Quentin and his family would be able to help her? Rescue her? Offer to adopt her?

Even with the broken glass cleaned up, her apartment was filthy and smelly, and she couldn't believe she'd let Quentin inside. She looked around the tiny space with total disgust and then realized that it was simply a reflection of her. However, there was no time to fix it now. She needed to focus on fixing herself first. At least good enough to make a decent appearance at Sapphire. If they were giving her the boot—and she expected they were—she could at least try to look respectable.

After starting Kendra's hangover remedy, Grace got into the shower and attempted to wash the cobwebs out of her head. Then she took her time doing her hair and makeup and finally dressed in an attractive yet relatively conservative outfit. If one was about to get fired, best to show up looking conventional and sedate, or at least that was her plan.

She downed one more small glass of orange juice before she went out the door, nervously chewing several pieces of mint gum as she started her car. As she drove toward Sapphire, she rehearsed the apology speech she would make to them. She wasn't exactly sure who "them" was, but at least she'd have a chance to say it to Mossy. She would confess in full that she had knowingly lied to him about her songwriting abilities. And she might even admit to having developed a bit of a drinking problem of late. She would lay all her ugly, embarrassing cards on the table.

As she entered Sapphire Music, going through security and then walking through the flashy lobby, she told herself to take it all in. This might be the last time she'd be able to do this. She paused to look at her own poster, shaking her head. Well, it was fun while it lasted. Okay, some of it was fun. A lot of it—maybe even most of it—was torture.

She rode up the elevator, practicing her lines in her head, but as the doors opened, she wondered why bother? If she was canned, she was canned. Why not just stop wasting every-body's time and quietly leave? Tuck her tail between her legs and crawl out like the whipped puppy she knew she was?

But once she got into Mossy's office, he didn't have the look of a man about to kick his client to the curb. In fact, he seemed rather pleased with himself as she sat down across from him. "You look slightly better than you did yesterday," he told her.

"Thanks . . . I guess."

"You were a little hard to get a hold of yesterday."

"So I heard."

"Everything okay?"

She frowned. *Was he nuts?*

"Sorry." He gave her what seemed like a smug smile. "But you will probably be feeling better as soon as you hear the news."

"What news?" She tilted her head to one side.

"The video . . ." He nodded. "It's doing all right."

"All right?" She studied him. "What does that mean?"

"It means it went viral, Gracie. It means we have one of the hottest videos on the web."

Grace tried to absorb this. The video went viral?

"And it means if the building chart holds, 'Misunderstood' just hit the top twenty."

"Airplay or downloads."

"Both."

She gave him a dejected nod as the truth of the moment slapped her in the face.

"That doesn't make you happy?"

She shrugged. "I'm happy for you . . . and for Sapphire."

"But you're not happy for yourself?" He looked completely perplexed.

"It just makes it official," she said slowly. "I'm a one-hit wonder just like my dad. Only it's not even my own song. It's *his*."

"Yeah, I had a long talk with Larry about that." He shuffled some papers in front of him. "And he decided that under the circumstances they don't want a follow-up song."

She sighed. Well, here it was, the final smackdown. She braced herself.

"Yep," Mossy said resolutely. "They want a full album."

Grace stared at him in confusion. Had she heard him wrong? "What?"

"He heard about your little meltdown, but I assured him you were fine." Mossy smiled. "We record when you get back."

"But . . . I don't understand. What . . . ?"

"Grace, they have writers! Larry would've brought them in sooner, but you kept saying you had songs!"

She still didn't completely get it. "I wanted to believe I could write songs," she confessed. "But the truth is, I can't. And I wouldn't blame them for dropping me."

"Drop you? Grace, aren't you listening? We're top twenty. Nobody's dropping you. You just can't write! Think about it, girl. Rhianna, Britney—they don't write either. They sing. And that's exactly what you're gonna do."

She was still trying to process this—they weren't giving her the boot? They were letting her make an album? With someone else's songs?

He slid a lyric sheet and a flash drive across his desk toward her. "This is your follow-up single. It's called 'One Fast Night' and it's brilliant. From one of Sapphire's guys, Alan Hobbs."

She picked them up, looking down at them in wonder. They were giving her another chance. It seemed too good to be true.

"Alan wrote it for Renae, but I talked Larry into giving it to you. Kills me we lose publishing, but I didn't have much choice. I'll have the rest of the songs when you get back. But learn this one on the road. Got it?" He peered at her.

"Yeah." She nodded as it continued to sink in.

"And I did book Randall to shoot the album cover. You're gonna have to trust me on that. He knows what sells."

She was too surprised and overwhelmed to question him.

"Hey, this is big, Gracie." He gave her a bright smile. "It's a once-in-a-lifetime opportunity. You just need to stay focused." He pointed a finger at her. "Don't fall apart like your dad."

She promised him she would keep it together, thanking him several times before he shooed her away. "I've got work to do," he said gruffly. "So do you."

Still feeling dazed by this strange turn of events, Grace got into the elevator and was about to press the down button but suddenly remembered something . . . rather someone. Quentin. She had to undo something. It had been a mistake to agree to go to dinner at his house. She'd been feeling weak and beaten, and she'd still been seriously hung over. Surely he wouldn't hold her to her commitment. She hit the up button, and as she rode the elevator up to the floor where she knew he worked, she prepared her excuses. Perhaps she would even begin by sharing her exciting news. She was just bursting out of the elevator when she nearly ran down the person coming in. Of course, it was Quentin.

"Oh, Quentin," she said in surprise. "I'm so sorry, but . . . something's come—"

"That did *not* just happen," he said with a big smile.

Something about seeing him like this, looking so thrilled to see her, she couldn't help but smile back at him.

"So, you doing okay now?" He gave her a concerned look.

"Yeah, I'm . . . I'm fine."

"Good. My parents are really stoked that you're coming over, Grace. My mom said she's even gonna try a new casserole." He grimaced slightly. "We'll see how that goes."

His eyes looked so sincere and his happiness so genuine, she couldn't bring herself to let him down. No, she decided, she was going to keep her word. She'd agreed to go and she would. "I just wanted to find out what time and get directions to your house," she said quietly. So he told her when and where, and Grace promised to be on time.

But as she drove home, she wished she could think of a believable excuse to bow out of this family dinner. The idea of sitting down to eat a meal with people who were probably a lot like her parents was truly disturbing. However, at the same time, the idea of disappointing Quentin was equally unsettling.

Back at her apartment, she distracted herself from her dinner plans by launching into a thorough cleaning of her apartment. By the time she finished, she realized it was nearly time to leave. And she had promised not to be late. She quickly freshened up, putting on another relatively conservative outfit. Then she hurried on down to her car and, following the directions he'd given her, she drove to Quentin's house.

Parked in the driveway, she suddenly felt unsure. What was she doing here? Why had she agreed to this? What difference would it make if she backed up and made a run for it? She could call and apologize later, saying how she was busy getting ready for her tour and learning her new song. All true.

She had just put the car in reverse when she observed Quentin emerge out the front door. Waving and smiling, he came out to welcome her. "There she is," he said as he opened her car door. "And just in time."

"In time for what?" she asked uneasily as she got out of her car.

"Hopefully a good dinner." He laughed. "But no guarantees."

She forced a smile as she looked up at a house that wasn't all that different from the one she'd shared with her parents until recently. Still, she didn't want to think about that, didn't want to be reminded of who and what she'd left behind. She took in a deep breath as they went inside—*Why had she come here?*

Quentin led her directly to the kitchen were she met his mother. She was just putting the finishing touches on a green salad.

"That looks good," Grace told Donna.

"According to some people, salads are my specialty." Donna laughed as she wiped her hands on a kitchen towel, pausing to peer curiously at Grace. "I'm so glad you could join us tonight," Donna said kindly. "I've been nagging Quentin to bring you home." She patted her son's back. "But I wasn't sure he could really deliver."

"Well, the temptation of a home-cooked meal . . ." Grace exchanged a knowing glance with Quentin. "How could I resist?"

"Did Quentin tell you about the time we heard your father back in Florida?"

"He mentioned that."

"Your father is such a gifted man." She gave Grace a warm smile. "And it seems the gift continues in you. Quentin tells me that you're about the hottest thing at Sapphire Music these days."

Grace tossed Quentin a questioning look. "I don't know about that. But I was pleased to hear they want me to tour."

"Well, of course they do," Donna declared.

Grace looked around the kitchen. Every counter seemed to be cluttered with bowls and ingredients, probably from whatever was in the oven. "Is there anything I can help you with in here."

Donna waved her hand. "No, no, the way I cook is a bit unorthodox." She pointed at Quentin. "Why don't you show Grace the rest of the house while I finish up a few things in here."

"Good idea." Quentin looked relieved as he led Grace out of the kitchen and patiently led her through the house. She suspected this impromptu tour had more to do with calming her nerves than showing her where they lived. Still, it was sweet.

"And this," Quentin opened the door to a cozy room with walls filled with bookshelves, "is my favorite room."

"Wow." Grace surveyed the hundreds of books. "You read all these?"

"Not all of them. Although my dad probably has. I hated reading when I was a kid. But eventually I learned to love it." He picked up a book from the desk, flipping through it with interest. "How about you?" He looked up. "You like to read?"

She remembered how she used to love to curl up with a good book, how she even used to take time to read the Bible. When was the last time she'd actually opened a book? "I used to read a lot," she admitted. "But now . . . well, I'm just so busy and everything."

He nodded as he set the book down. "Well, you'll definitely have time on tour. All those long boring bus rides, right?" He looked at the bookshelf by the desk. "I'll pick out a good one for you to take." He grinned. "Just in case you find out you have time to read again."

"Hello in there." A tall, gray-haired man peered in the door. "This a private party or can I join you?"

Quentin laughed. "Come on in, Dad. Meet Grace Trey." More introductions were made, and Grace nervously shook his hand. She wasn't sure why she felt so uneasy since both of Quentin's parents were perfectly pleasant and kind. And yet she knew they were church people. She knew they could find reason to judge her if they wanted. What if they knew how totally wasted she'd been only yesterday? Or if they realized how she rocked the house when she performed in a club or, perhaps worst of all, if they knew how she'd run away from home. She felt certain that, if they knew her better, they wouldn't approve of their son's friendship with her.

"Well, you've grown up some since we last saw you," Rick told her. "But it sounds as if your music career is really taking off."

"Dinner!" Donna called out.

Relieved for a distraction from talking about her "music career," Grace decided to use this opportunity to ask Quentin about himself. As they were seated, she turned her attention onto him. "As long as I've known you, I've never really heard why you're interning at Sapphire Music," she said as she placed the linen napkin in her lap.

"I've always loved music," he told her as his mom set a large, crusty-looking casserole on the table. "I used to play all the time."

"That's for sure," Donna told Grace as she sat down. "Quentin and his buddies thought they were going to be the next Backstreet Boys."

"Not exactly, Mom." Quentin laughed nervously.

"Well, they did make plenty of racket in the bonus room above the garage," Rick confided to Grace. "I had to get myself a set of headphones just to hear myself think."

"Oh, it wasn't that bad," Donna defended her son. She tipped her head to Rick now. "Ready to pray?"

He nodded, outstretching his hands to her and Quentin. Donna reached for Grace's other hand. Feeling awkward and yet strangely comforted at the same time, Grace held Quentin's parents' hands, bowing her head while Rick asked a blessing for their meal. The prayer wasn't all that different from the way her dad prayed before meals, but at the same time it felt foreign . . . or like a land she'd left far behind her. A land that she'd been missing far more than she cared to admit.

"Amen," Rick declared. Grace's hands were gently squeezed then released.

"Yeah," Quentin linked eyes with Grace, "a blessing becomes even more critical on nights when Mom's experimenting with a new recipe."

Rick chuckled, and Donna just wrinkled her nose at her son. "Would you like me to serve you?" she asked Grace.

"Thank you." Grace made a nervous smile. "That looks good."

As Grace handed Donna her plate, she turned her attention back on Quentin. "So you said that you love music," she began, "is that why you're at Sapphire? Are you trying to launch your music career too?"

"No, it didn't take long for me to figure out that I wasn't very good." He handed his empty plate to his mom. "But I still love music, and I still want a career that involves music. In college I discovered I have a pretty good head for business. So I thought I might try going the executive route. It seemed like a good fit."

"And at Sapphire . . . that's very cool," Grace told him.

"Yeah, I couldn't believe it when I landed an internship there. I mean Sapphire Music is where everyone wants to work. I was really stoked."

"It's a great opportunity," Grace said as she put some salad on her salad plate.

"So . . . tell us about this concert tour you're doing," Rick said to Grace.

"Oh, it's not really a concert tour," she explained. "It's more like a promo thing. Just doing local radio shows and stuff."

"That sounds exciting," Donna said as she passed Grace the basket of bread.

"Yeah, I'm looking forward to it. Plus, I just found out I'm doing an album when I get back."

"Hey, congratulations." Rick handed the butter dish to Grace.

"Thanks. It's crazy." Grace looked around the table, and seeing that everyone had been served, she forked into the casserole.

"I hadn't even heard that news yet." Quentin gave her a curious look, and suddenly she remembered how he'd found her this morning . . . hung over, desperate and pathetic. What must he be thinking?

"Yeah, well, you know this industry," she said lightly. "Everything is constantly changing. Hard to keep up." She put the bite into her mouth, taking her time to chew and savor the taste. "This is good," she told Donna.

Quentin tossed Grace a questioning look.

"It really is," she assured him. "I like it a lot."

Donna beamed at her. "I just knew you'd enjoy a home-cooked meal," she told her. "That's exactly what I told Quentin."

"You were right." Grace forked into her salad, noticing that there was no dressing on it but not wanting to mention it. Mostly she wanted this meal to get over with as quickly as possible, and then she would be on her way.

"It must've been a bit scary to leave your mom and dad behind . . . to move out here all by yourself." Donna's brow creased as she buttered a slice of bread.

"Yeah . . . uh, definitely." Grace tried to think of a comfortable answer that wasn't a lie. "But an opportunity came up for me to do it, and it seemed like . . ." She glanced over at Quentin, remembering his comment about his internship. *"A good fit."* Okay, so she wasn't original, but at least she was being somewhat honest. She wanted to be honest with these good people. They deserved that much from her.

"Well, it sounds like you're making the most of it," Donna told her. "Good for you!"

Grace gave Donna a grateful smile.

"Oh, dear, I forgot the salad dressing," Donna said suddenly. "Excuse me a minute."

"So, how's your dad doing?" Rick asked Grace while Donna was in the kitchen.

"Oh, he's . . . he's good."

"Still speaking at churches?"

"No, he's a full-time music pastor now." She really didn't want to go there, but how could she change course without being rude?

"That's in Alabama, right?"

"Yeah, outside of Birmingham."

Donna came back with a bottle of homemade dressing, handing it to Grace. "There you go, dear. It's a creamy Italian. Unless you'd like something different. I have—"

"No, no, it's just fine," Grace assured her.

"Your dad and I had a great talk that night," Rick continued. "After you guys finished playing. What a heart that man has for the Lord . . . and such a love for people."

Grace forced a still smile as she poured some dressing on her salad.

"And I'm sure you already heard that was a big night for Quentin," Donna told Grace.

Grace peered curiously at Quentin, and suddenly he looked almost as uncomfortable as she felt.

"I'll tell you later," he said quietly.

Now Rick launched into a story about the time Quentin booked a gig for his band. "It was only a middle-school dance, but they assumed the band could actually play."

"We could play," Quentin insisted. "Just not very well."

"Well, at least you did the right thing, son." Rick chuckled.

"We gave them back their money," Quentin sheepishly told Grace. Now everyone laughed. More stories were told, followed by more laughter, and despite herself, Grace realized she was having a pretty good time. Who would've thought? But the goodness was tinged with sadness because they reminded her of her own family. And that was something she did not want to think about.

# Chapter 21

**W**hen it was finally time to call it a night and go home, Grace was almost reluctant to leave. After she'd gotten over her fears and anxiety, Quentin and his family had started to feel like a warm, safe haven in the midst of a crazy storm. Not so different from her own family way back when. Back before Grace had gotten serious about her own music, back before she'd run away and torn them apart.

Trying to block out the darker thoughts, Grace thanked Quentin's parents for a lovely evening and, at Donna's urging, even promised to come back again someday. Although she wasn't sure that was ever going to happen. Especially if they learned more about her . . . if they ever found out what she'd done to her parents. As she got her purse, Quentin insisted on walking her to her car. And once they were outside, she knew there was something she wanted to ask him. She just wasn't quite sure how.

"I've been thinking about something," she said as they stood by her car.

"Yeah?" He leaned toward her with genuine interest.

She blinked. Did he think she was about to declare her love for him? "It has to do with something your dad said."

"Oh?" Now he leaned back a little, but he still looked interested. "What's that?"

"He was talking about when you guys went to see my dad and how that was a big night for you . . . back in Florida. I was just curious."

"Oh, yeah, my big night." He nodded with a faraway look, as if remembering.

"How old were you then?" she asked as she leaned against the hood of the car.

"Eighteen." Standing next to her, he leaned against the hood too. "To be honest, I can't even remember why I went. My parents didn't try to make me. Probably good since I wouldn't have listened if they had. I was a punk."

"That's hard to imagine."

"It's true. And I don't even remember exactly what your dad said that night. Except that it shook me. Made me rethink my whole life." He exhaled and looked up at the sky, which was surprisingly clear tonight. Grace could actually see some stars. "Anyway, when we got home, I told my parents I wasn't a Christian. I knew the facts and everything, but it wasn't real for me. You know?"

She wasn't sure that she did know—did she really know anything?

"Guess your dad's words got me." Quentin shoved his hands in his pockets. "To be more honest, *God* got to me. But he did use your dad to get my attention. That's one reason I feel grateful for your dad."

She shrugged, trying to act nonchalant but at the same time wondering why it always came back to this—why couldn't she just leave her dad and her past behind? Why did it feel like he was trailing her, shadowing her every step?

"Grace, I got to ask you," he began in a gentle but probing tone. "And you totally don't have to answer if you don't want to. But what happened between you and your dad?"

She sighed and looked away.

"Why are you really out here?" he continued. "Are you running to something, or are you simply running away?"

She looked back at him now, evenly taking in the handsome features of his face. He really was a nice guy, just a bit too inquisitive. "Tell your parents thanks again," she stiffly told him. "I had a nice time." Then she got into her car and drove away. Keeping her full attention on the road, she tried to push the last part of their conversation into some dark corner of her mind.

But even after she got home, safely tucked into her recently cleaned apartment, Quentin's words continued to haunt her. At first she was mad at him, wanting to demand what right he had to question her like that. But then she felt somewhat relieved that he could actually see through her, almost as if he was trying to understand her in order to help. But then she felt angry all over again. Why did Quentin insist on prying into her world, rocking her boat? Didn't he get what kind of pressure she was under? Didn't he understand that she took her music seriously? That she had sacrificed nearly everything to reach this place? Running from something? *Really?*

Then she thought about the kind words Quentin and his parents had for her dad. And she knew her dad wasn't a monster. He didn't deserve to be completely written out of her life. And yet, wasn't that what he wanted? Wasn't that the message he had sent her: "My way or the highway." Still, she knew she owed so much to him. And she knew that—despite everything, despite their differences, despite their fights—her father loved her. She knew it.

She picked up her phone and pushed what used to be one of her most commonly used speed dial numbers, right below Rachel's. The word *Home* appeared on the screen. She stared at the familiar letters and considered pushing *Send*, but something inside of her would not let her do it. She tossed the phone aside and went to bed.

Grace frowned up at the tour bus, watching as the guys loaded the holds with instrument cases and luggage and crates. She knew she should be excited—over the moon—to know that her tour was about to begin. But all she felt was numb . . . and slightly lost. She wasn't even sure why.

"What is it?" Mossy asked her for the second time. "What's wrong now?"

"Nothing." She shook her head.

"Then why are you acting like this?" he demanded.

"It's nothing," she insisted. "Just . . . well, I have a lot on my mind. No big deal."

"It is a big deal," he told her. "This tour's a big deal, Gracie. A lot's riding on this. You *need* to stay sharp."

"I will!" she snapped at him.

"Look, Gracie," he softened his tone, "I'd go with you, but—"

"Mossy, I'm fine! Really."

"All right." He tipped his head toward the bus. "They should have your itinerary and—"

"I got it," she waved the papers in his face. "I'm on it, Mossy. You can trust me, okay?"

"Okay." He gave her an uncertain look. "Well, just don't forget to learn your new song. We'll schedule for—"

"I know, I know," she told him. "You've told me like a hundred times." She almost added, "just like my dad used to do," but stopped herself. That was just way too close to home.

He held up his hands in a helpless gesture. "Okay. You're on it. I get it."

She forced a smile. "Thanks, Moss. See ya."

"Rock on," he called out as she got onto the bus.

She just nodded and waved. Sometimes Mossy was an awful lot like her dad. And then at other times they were as different as night and day. Gracie made her way past the driver's area to where Kendra was sitting on the couch across from the kitchen area. She looked uneasy, as if this was about to get awkward. Grace pressed her lips together as she studied her, unsure of what to say.

"Gracie," Kendra began, "I just want to—"

"It's okay," Grace acted nonchalant. "We're cool." She pointed to the chair across from Kendra. "Anyone sitting there?"

"Just you." Kendra looked relieved.

Grace forced yet another smile and sat. "So when do we leave?" she asked.

"Who knows?" Kendra sighed. "Just when you think we're ready to roll, someone remembers something. It could take five minutes or thirty."

Grace heard a tapping sound behind her and turned to see Quentin outside, tapping on her window with an urgent expression.

Grace just shook her head as she stood. "Don't let 'em leave without me," she told Kendra as she made her way back outside. Thankfully Mossy was gone now.

"Quentin," she said casually as she went over to him. "What's up?"

"I was hoping you hadn't left yet," he told her.

"I think we're about to." She studied his eyes. They always had such a genuinely sincere look about them, as if she could truly trust him. And yet she didn't want to. More and more Quentin reminded her of everything she'd left behind . . . and of everything she wasn't.

"I brought you something." He held a paper bag out to her.

She peeked inside. "Your mom's cookies!"

"And a few other goodies too. I know how you forget to eat sometimes."

Now she pulled out a paperback book and stared at it.

"Remember we thought you'd have time to read on the tour?" he said.

She held up the book, pointing at the author's name on the front cover and laughed. "*That's* my pastor."

"*What?*"

"Well, my parents' pastor anyway." She frowned down at the familiar words on the cover—*Own It! Is it Really Your Faith?* by Tim Bryant.

"Are you serious?" Quentin flipped the book over to where Pastor Tim's pleasant face smiled from the back cover.

"I am." She folded her arms across her front, glancing over at the bus, which still didn't look close to leaving.

"Tim Bryant is your pastor?"

She shrugged. "Yeah, I guess."

Quentin slapped the book onto his forehead. "Oh, yeah. Of course. My parents got this book when you guys came to our church. I thought I was being so clever, but instead I'm such a moron."

"No," she shook her head. "It's . . . well, thank you."

"Have you already read it?"

She sheepishly shook her head. "No, not yet."

"It's really good," he said gently. "Okay, it changed my life. Anyway, hope you like it." He pressed the book into her hands. "Maybe we can talk about it, you know, when you get back."

She sighed. "Yeah, maybe. But I better go now." She nodded over to where the guys were starting to close the holds beneath the bus, loudly slamming them shut. "Looks like we're almost ready to roll."

"I'll be praying you have a good trip," he told her, his eyes locked on hers.

"Thanks," she mumbled, turning away. Why did it always feel like he was looking right through her? Like he could strip all her phoniness away and see her for who she was, and yet it didn't seem to be driving him away. "See ya," she called as she boarded the bus again.

Making her way back to her seat, Grace slipped the book into her bag, but she could feel Kendra's eyes on her.

"What was that all about?" Kendra asked in a slightly teasing tone.

"Nothing." Grace crossed one leg over the other and returned Kendra's gaze.

"Looked like something to me."

Grace looked away as the bus began to move, pretending to be focused on the Sapphire building as they slowly moved through the back parking lot. She wasn't angry at Kendra anymore, but she was going to be more careful with their friendship from now on. Kendra might be a good stylist, but Grace knew her well enough to know that she might not always have Grace's best interests at heart. If Grace was going to survive and succeed in this business, she needed to get smarter. A lot smarter.

Grace enjoyed looking out the window as they drove through the dessert. It was so different from the landscape she'd grown up with in the south—vast and barren, it almost seemed endless. She felt small and slightly lost in the midst of it. However, she suspected it wasn't just the landscape that was making her feel like this.

To distract herself, she studied the itinerary. It looked like they had a lot of ground to cover in just a couple of weeks. Heading east, they had dozens of stops in dozens of cities. Mossy was right, she would need to stay focused. She flipped to the last page of the itinerary and was surprised to see they would even tour the South. Her eyes continued down the list: Springfield and Saint Louis, Missouri; Louisville, Kentucky— she stopped and stared in disbelief—they were even stopping in

Birmingham, Alabama, just thirty minutes from her parents' home. She closed the itinerary, shoving it into her bag. Well, in all likelihood, her parents wouldn't hear about her tour. And even if they did, she felt certain they would not come.

Their first stop was Flagstaff, Arizona. A college town with Old West charm, Grace happily trekked into the radio station with some of the musicians. While they set up, Grace was interviewed by the DJ.

"So there you have it," he said as they were finishing up. "Gracie Trey is a name you're going to be hearing a lot about in the future. And now she and her band are going to play her new hit—well, I guess it's kind of an old hit done in a fresh, new way. Don't go away, listeners, you're in for a real treat."

They played "Misunderstood" with enthusiasm. Then, as the guys packed it up, she autographed some photos for a few fans who had stopped by the station. Then she and her crew toured the town a bit and got some lunch, and then they were back on the road again.

So it went for the next couple of days. Driving, stopping, talking, playing, autographing—and then back on the road again. During her interview in Salt Lake City, the DJ made an exciting announcement: "I was just online," he told Grace, "and it looks like 'Misunderstood' just hit number fourteen on the Top Forty Chart."

"Seriously?" Her eyes grew big.

"According to *Billboard*," he told her. "And they should know."

"That's awesome!" She exchanged a high five with him.

"Congratulations," he told her.

After the interview she and the band performed, and when they finished and excited the station, they were greeted by dozens of fans. Kendra handed Grace photos to sign; and, even though she was tired, Grace tried to say at least a few personal words to each one. However, one girl caught Grace's eye. She appeared to be about ten, standing in line with her father, anxiously waiting for her turn. Finally the pair stepped up. "What's your name?" Grace asked the girl.

"Hannah." The girl smiled up with eager blue eyes. "I love how you sing."

"Thank you!" Grace wrote '*to Hannah*' on the top of the photo. "What do you like to do?" she asked her. "Like hobbies, you know?"

"I love to sing," Hannah said shyly.

Grace grinned as she wrote, "keep on singing!" and signed her name. "Good for you, Hannah. I loved to sing when I was your age too."

"We had to get Hannah excused from school to meet you," the dad told her. "But I think it's worth it. You're a real inspiration."

Hannah beamed up at her dad.

"Well, thanks for coming," Grace told them. She pointed at Hannah. "And I mean it, keep on singing and who knows . . ." She waved her arms. "This all might be yours someday."

The dad laughed. "Wouldn't that be something, Hannah?"

As they went on their way, Grace looked longingly at them. It was like going back in time, like she was seeing herself . . . and her dad . . . back when they used to get along. She swallowed the lump in her throat as she signed the next photograph. Forcing a smile, she cheerfully greeted the rest of the fans. But once she got on the bus, she went back to her bed and, sliding the curtain closed, she cried.

In between stops Grace had plenty of time to learn and practice her new song. And although she knew she needed to perform it like she really believed it, the more she played it the less she liked it. She also had enough time to start reading Pastor Tim's book. And, perhaps most important, Grace had lots of time to think . . . really think.

In Tulsa, Oklahoma, Grace was stunned to see how many fans were lined up at the radio station. It was only eight o'clock in the morning, and judging by the length of the line, some of them had been there awhile.

"What's going on?" she asked Kendra as she finished doing Grace's hair.

"*You're* going on," Kendra teased.

"I know. But so many fans, are they really here for me?"

"When your song hits number three on the charts, you should expect some—"

"*Number three?*" Grace stared at Kendra. "Seriously?"

"Yeah. I just read it online this morning. Hadn't you heard?"

"No." Grace just shook her head. "That's amazing."

"I'll bet you they're throwing a party at Sapphire," Kendra said as she brushed some blush onto Grace's cheeks.

After the stop in Tulsa, Grace opened up her laptop; and after reading the blurbs about her song hitting number three, she checked e-mail and was surprised to see that her mom had written. Eager to see what was up, she clicked onto it and read.

> *Dear Grace,*
>
> *I know you probably won't have time to answer this, but I wanted to let you know Dad and I have been following your career and your tour. We know you'll be in Birmingham next week, and we would love to drive over to see you. Would you mind if we came?*
>
> *Love,*
> *Mom*

Grace read and reread the post; and then, without answering, she shut down her laptop and shoved it into the drawer next to the bed. Part of her was happy to hear from Mom. Another part of her felt uneasy . . . bordering on angry. Mom wasn't just asking for herself—she was asking for Dad too. Did Dad assume that he could just waltz back into her life as if nothing had ever happened? Or did he plan to confront her and lay out all her faults for everyone to see? Even if he wanted to let bygones be bygones, and that seemed unlikely, Grace wasn't ready for that.

Eager for a distraction from her mom's e-mail, she picked up Pastor Tim's book, flipping over to where she'd left off about midway through. Of course, as fate—or God—would have it, the chapter was about forgiveness. His point, and she'd heard it before, was that God expected her to forgive others the same way He'd forgiven her—totally.

She closed the book and reached for her computer. Okay, she could take this step toward forgiveness. It didn't mean that she'd gone the whole distance, but she could at least make an effort. She opened Mom's e-mail and wrote a brief reply, letting her know that it would be fine for them to come. But she grimaced as she hit *Send*. This could be such a mistake, not to mention embarrassing. And yet, it would be good to see her parents again—hard, yes, but good.

Thanks to "Misunderstood"'s unexpected hop to the top of the charts, the radio tour had morphed into a slightly bigger tour, including a number of TV appearances in some of the larger cities. Including Birmingham.

Grace woke up early that morning. Sitting in her chair not far from the driver's seat, she stared out the front window as the sunrise illuminated the sky. But when she saw the "Welcome to Birmingham" sign, her stomach started to tie itself into knots.

"Come on, Gracie," Kendra called from the back. "We got about forty-five minutes to get you ready for the morning show."

Some of the band members were starting to stir now. Grace squeezed past the bass player as she went to the bedroom in back. Feeling anxious and slightly lost, she watched as Kendra laid out some clothes for her. Thankfully it was an outfit she wouldn't feel embarrassed to be wearing when she met with her parents—that is, if they showed. She was starting to wonder if they really would come. After all, it was one thing for Mom to want to see Grace. Dad was an entirely different story. He might dig in his heels and insist they stay home. It wouldn't surprise her.

"So you think your folks are coming today?" Kendra asked quietly as she rolled Grace's hair onto the curling tool.

"I don't know."

"Do you want to see them?"

Grace shrugged. "I'm not sure."

"Nervous about the show?"

She shrugged again.

"Well, you'll be fine," Kendra assured her. "Just be yourself."

"Right." Grace didn't know how to tell Kendra she wasn't entirely sure how to do that—how could she be herself when she felt so lost so much of the time?

Grace still felt uneasy as they went into the studio. But when the assistant led them all to the green room, Grace tried to appear relaxed by settling into a chair against the wall and reading a copy of *Variety*. Meanwhile her band members, oblivious to her nerves, joked and drank coffee and visited among themselves.

Of course, the first article to catch her eye was about how she and her dad were the first father and daughter to score a top-five hit with the same song. It figured. She heard the door to the green room open and supposed it was time for them to go get set up. She set down the magazine and looked to see that as her bandmates were exiting the room, some other people were coming in.

Her heart lurched inside of her chest to see her parents walking into the room. Accompanied by Pastor Tim and Sharon, they all looked so familiar . . . and yet so out of place. A mixture of shock and fear and happiness surged through her as she braced herself, standing to greet them.

# Chapter 22

Taking a steadying breath and trying to conceal how totally unsettling this felt, Grace slowly moved toward her mom, forcing a nervous smile to her lips.

"Hey, baby." Mom gazed at her with misty eyes, opening out her arms.

Then, just like that, she and Mom were hugging tightly, and it was like neither of them wanted to let go. As they embraced, Grace could see her father from the corner of her eye. He stood nearby with lips pressed tightly together, as if he wasn't quite sure what to do with himself. Or perhaps he wished he hadn't come.

"It's so great to see you," Mom said when she finally released Grace. "You look good."

Dad continued standing there like his shoes were nailed to the floor, awkwardly watching, but not saying a word.

"Thanks," Grace told Mom. "And thanks for coming." She smiled at the Bryants now. "Good to see you guys."

"You too, Grace," Pastor Tim beamed at her. "We just wanted to say hi."

"If you'll excuse us, we're gonna grab something to drink," Sharon told her. "Let you guys catch up."

Grace just nodded, forcing a nervous smile.

"Actually," Mom went over to join Sharon and Tim. "I think I'll go with you. I'd like to get some coffee." She smiled at Grace. "I'll see you after, okay?"

Although this felt like a setup, Grace tried to act natural. And judging by her dad's face, he was just as surprised as she was by this. They'd both been blindsided. She just stared at him now, wondering what she was supposed to say or do . . . and wishing it wasn't so awkward.

"So . . . I guess since we're part of music history now," he began slowly, but his words sounded sincere. "I want to say congratulations, Grace."

She made a small smile. "Yeah, you too."

His serious expression softened as he studied her. "So, *how are you?*"

"I'm good."

"Mossy treating you okay?" His tone sounded more fatherly now, and it sounded surprisingly good to her.

"Yeah, I guess."

"I watched your video." Dad looked at her now—looked at her as if he was truly seeing her. He smiled, but his eyes were still sad. "It made me realize—maybe I never really gave you the credit that I should have." He sighed. "You've been gifted in ways I can't even begin to describe, Grace."

He paused now, running his fingers through his hair, the way he did when he was really nervous, then continued as if he was worried he wouldn't get it all out. "I think somewhere, deep down I always knew it. And maybe that's why in my heart I never really wanted you to grow up. Never gave you any space. 'Cause nothing made me happier than playing music. With you."

He gave her a sweet, humble smile, and she felt her heart melting. Those times playing music with Dad had been her happiest times too.

"But right now, I'm just glad you're safe." His eyes were starting to tear up, and there was a big lump in her throat too. He took in a deep breath, then looked at her guitar, which was leaning in a stand near the rest of the band's instruments. He reached for it and stroked the wood—the same way she did sometimes—and smiled. "Still using this old thing?"

Grace knew she was on the verge of tears. Swallowing hard, she tried to keep her voice even. "I guess it's got me this far."

He tested the guitar now, slowly playing the chords of "It Is Well with My Soul"—the same hymn they'd played together the day he'd given her that guitar for her eighth birthday. But he only played a few bars before he stopped playing. "Still sounds good."

She nodded, blinking to hold back tears. "Keep playing," she said in a husky voice.

As he continued to play, she reached for her bandmate's guitar and started to play along with him. With eyes locked, they played "It Is Well" together—just as if they'd been practicing this song for years. And hadn't they?

Before they could finish, the band members burst back into the green room. "We're on," the bass player announced as he grabbed up his bass. With eyes still on Dad, Grace stopped playing and handed her bandmate his guitar. With tear-filled eyes, her dad handed her back her guitar, then tipped his head and smiled—as if he was telling her to go out there and rock the house.

Taking the guitar from him, she went out to where she and her band were herded to a recording area, and before long they were all playing "Misunderstood" with so much enthusiasm that no one would've guessed they'd done it just like this a hundred times before. Grace could see her parents and the Bryants through the soundproof glass, but it was her father's face that she could not take her eyes off. And when they finished the song, he gave her a smile that seemed to say it all—he was proud of her.

Outside in the parking lot, after she'd signed photos and chatted with fans, her parents and the Bryants remained outside of the bus to say good-bye.

"So where you headed now?" her dad asked her.

"Couple of stops in Texas, then, I think, Phoenix. Then back to LA. There might be more. I don't really remember."

"It's so good to see you, sweetheart." Mom hugged her again.

"Good to see you." Now she looked at her dad. "Good to see you too." Everything in her wanted to hug him, but it was like she was stuck. Her feet would not budge. She wished he'd make the first step, but when he didn't, she turned to the Bryants. "I should go," she said to them. "Thanks for coming."

"You take care," Sharon told her.

"Nice seeing you, Grace." Tim grasped her hand, giving it a warm squeeze.

Grace forced a smile, waving to all of them as she headed for the bus. "By the way, Pastor Tim," she called from the steps. "Your book, it's really good."

Tim looked shocked as he nodded. "Thanks, Grace."

As she went inside the bus, she could see that her parents and the Bryants were all slightly dumbfounded by her last statement. What—did they think she'd forgotten how to read? She smiled sadly to herself as she watched her dad slipping an arm around Mom. His face was a mixture of emotions, and she suspected he was holding onto Mom just to keep from falling over. But as the diesel engine roared to life and the bus pulled out of the parking lot, she was the one who broke down in tears.

# Chapter 23

**G**race felt completely exhausted when the tour ended. In fact, if it had lasted one day longer, she felt certain she would've come undone. It was already dark as she dragged her wheeled bag down the corridor to her apartment. As she pulled out her key, all she could think about was bed. She wanted to fall into bed and sleep for a week.

She paused by her apartment door to see something white sitting on the floor. A small glass vase with three perfect lilies. She picked up the humble bouquet and removed the card, reading it to herself by the dim hall light. Despite her fatigue she couldn't help but smile at Quentin's unexpected thoughtfulness. What a guy!

Carrying the vase inside, Grace set it on the dining room table and admired it briefly. Then, without even bothering to unpack her bag or remove her clothes, she collapsed onto her bed and fell fast asleep.

When Grace woke up, the sun was pouring through her window, and her phone was ringing. Disoriented, she tried to remember where she was—not the bus—and slowly getting her bearings, she located her purse and finally her phone in time to see that it was Mossy. First he welcomed her home, and then he said he wanted to see her in his office. She knew that it was related to the e-mail she'd sent him a few days ago—an e-mail he hadn't even responded to.

"Gotta go," he said before she could try to get him to talk about it on the phone. "See you in an hour or so?"

"Sure," she said a bit grumpily. "See ya."

It took her nearly an hour to shower and dress and make herself presentable enough to go out in public. It was weird, she thought as she picked up her purse. She used to be able to get ready so much faster. But, thanks to Kendra's perfectionist ways, Grace was much more conscious of her looks nowadays.

"Your appearance is a big part of your ticket," Kendra had told her often enough. "You need to remember that wherever you go, people are looking."

She checked her mirror once more before she walked out the door. For the conversation she planned to have with Mossy this afternoon, she needed to feel confident and strong and persuasive. Considering how tired she still felt from the tour, it would not be easy. Besides that, she knew Mossy and how he worked. He would try to manipulate her to get his way. But she was not going to back down on this.

Her resolve grew firmer as she walked through the lobby at Sapphire. Seeing her poster up there, her video playing on a couple of the big screens, knowing her song had nearly topped the charts—all of it helped to bolster her confidence. Mossy would have to listen to her. She would make him.

She was barely in his office when she could see that he was angry. Oh, sure, he was sitting calmly behind his desk, his hands twirling a pen between his fingers, but his eyes were as dark as a summertime thunderstorm. "Where is this coming from?" he demanded as soon as she sat down.

"I just don't like the song." She set the flash drive on his desk.

"But it's a hit, Gracie!"

"I don't care. It's all about manipulating a guy and a one-night stand. Why can't we just pick another one?"

"I have picked other ones! Eleven others! All of which are going on your album." He pointed to the flash drive. "Including this one, which is your follow-up single!"

"You're not listening, Mossy. I'm not singing it!"

Mossy's hands curled into fists of frustration as he glared at her. "You sound so much like your dad right now. It's sick!"

"What's the big deal? It's one song! And leave my dad out of it."

Mossy's face registered his surprise. He wasn't used to hearing her defending her dad. "Well, I talked to Larry this morning," he said in a way that suggested he was holding all the right cards.

"About what?"

"He didn't want me to tell you."

"Tell me what?"

"We got it. You're opening for Renae."

Grace was blown away. It was really happening. "She picked me?"

"She picked you."

So it was true. She was going to open for Renae Taylor. This had been her dream for so long. But even so, did it mean she had to compromise on this? Didn't she have any rights in this business?

"So, whatever's running around in your head, you need to get past it. These are the songs Sapphire wants, and these are the songs you're gonna deliver."

Grace wasn't really processing his words now. She was stuck on the fact that she would be opening for Renae. They would be touring together. This was big. Really big.

"You mean it?" she said again, "I'm really opening for Renae Taylor?"

"Yes." He nodded. "Because you *are* the next Renae Taylor."

She felt torn again. Was she just going to roll over because he was promising her this bone? Although Renae Taylor was a pretty big bone.

"So you're gonna go in the studio and nail the album," he said calmly, persuasively. "Then you'll do the photo shoot with Randall, just as planned. And you know why?" His lips curled into a knowing smile. "Because *this* is why you came out here. *This* is what you were born to do. Grace. *You made it.*"

Grace took in a slow, deep breath. She knew she was tired. More than tired. She was exhausted and fatigued. It was possible that she hadn't been thinking about these things clearly enough. This was her career . . . and headlining with Renae. How could she turn her back on that? She glanced at the prominent plaque hanging behind Mossy's head. Johnny Trey's gold record for "Misunderstood." Soon hers would be hanging next to it. "I gotta think about this," she said tiredly as she stood.

"Yeah, you do that. Think about how hard you've worked for this, Gracie. Think about what it's going to feel like to open for Renae . . . to become the next Renae." He stood and smiled. "You think about it."

Grace drove her car to Malibu, where she could walk on the beach and clear her head and just think. But as soon she got out of her car, her phone rang. *Please, don't be Mossy*, she thought as she reached for it. To her relief it was Quentin. "Hey," she said softly. "Thanks for the flowers."

"Sure. Welcome home, rock star."

"Thanks, I guess."

"You guess?"

"Oh, Quentin, I'm so confused." Now she explained her conflict with Mossy. "I came down to the beach . . . you know . . . to sort it all out."

"Which beach?"

"Malibu."

"Hey, I'm not far from there. Want company?"

"Sure. That'd be great."

Before long they were walking down the sunny beach together, and she was pouring out her heart to him, not holding anything back. Somehow she knew he would understand. After all, he worked for Sapphire too. He knew what she was up against.

"And it's not just the songs," she said finally. "It's everything."

"Grace," he said calmly. "You don't *have* to do it."

"Quentin, I'm opening for Renae Taylor! I can't blow this. Mossy's right, this is why I came out here. I should be so happy right now. What's wrong with me?"

"Grace," he said gently, *"you already know."*

She frowned at him. And now they both just walked in silence for awhile. She understood what he was saying to her, but it wasn't the words she wanted to hear. Or maybe it was. "I'm so confused," she confessed. "One minute I think I know what I want. The next minute I'm questioning myself."

"Maybe you should question yourself," he said quietly. "*Why* do you want a music career? Why do you want *any* of it—the fame, the success, the money? If you just want it for yourself, there's always going to be something missing. You'll never be satisfied with it."

"You sound like my dad." She gave him a half smile.

"Wow, thanks."

Grace knew that he meant it sincerely, and for a nice change it didn't bother her to hear him speaking so fondly about her dad. It was actually kind of sweet.

"But Mossy is right, Grace."

She blinked in surprise. Quentin was agreeing with Mossy?

"You could make a million albums. You could be bigger than Renae. It's all completely possible . . . within your reach." He stopped walking and peered directly into her eyes. "But none of it matters if you're not doing it for God."

She let out a long sigh.

"Did you read the book, Grace?"

She simply nodded. "Yeah."

"You think maybe it's like your pastor says? We know it in our heads. But we don't *own it?* Is Jesus Christ really who you're living for, Grace?"

She bit her lip as she considered this. At one time she'd believed Jesus was in her heart. But that was a long time ago. It seemed like she'd left Him behind . . . along with everyone else she'd loved.

"'Cause maybe the problems you've had with your dad . . . maybe they just reflect your relationship with God." He shrugged. "That was my story anyway."

She knew that was her story too, but she wasn't ready to admit it. She wasn't ready to *own it.*

"Look," Quentin said kindly but firmly. "Go ahead and open for Renae. Or don't open for her. That's not what matters right now. Get your life right with God, Grace. And then make things right with your dad. Until you do that, you'll never find what you're really looking for."

Grace just stared at him. Most of her knew he was right. Most of her wanted to agree with him. But another part of her wasn't ready to let go of the dream she'd been chasing so hard, the dream that was finally starting to come true.

Why did everything have to be so hard?

Later that night Grace paced back and forth in her apartment, going from the kitchen to the living room and to her bedroom, over and over and again. Somehow she had to make sense of this—she had to figure out her life . . . her music career. Really, it shouldn't be this difficult. Except that it was. It seemed impossible to decide, like her mind was split right down the middle.

As she gazed out her bedroom window, looking past the darkened street to where the illuminated cross glowed from the peak of the church, she was ready to call Mossy. She would politely tell him to forget it. She would refuse to lower her standards to appease him. She knew she'd been on what her dad would call the *slippery slope*—if she did not get off, she would probably crash before long. And what about the recent gossip she'd read about Renae Taylor, claiming the star needed to go to alcohol rehab? Was that where Grace wanted to wind up? She marched into the kitchen and took the last bottle of vodka, emptying its contents into the sink. *There!*

But as she walked back through the living room, she paused to gaze at the Sapphire poster pinned above her couch—Gracie Trey, rocker chick in all her glory. She sighed. Could she really kiss that good-bye and walk away? After all, this was the big break she'd been waiting for. Opening for Renae Taylor was not to be taken lightly.

Now she noticed Randall's photography book lying on the floor by the couch. Was that really the way she wanted to be portrayed? She flipped through the pages with disgust. Even the girls who had on clothes looked skanky. She'd heard Kendra say it enough times—it wasn't enough to be talented, Sapphire wanted the *whole* package, and everyone knew that sexy was highly marketable. But was Grace willing to compromise herself to do this?

She dropped the book back to the floor with a thud, then went over to the table where she'd set the lyrics to the song she'd argued with Mossy over. She read through the lines, just shaking her head in dismay. How could she sing those words and pretend it was okay? She tossed the lyrics down. It was all wrong and she knew it.

At least she knew it in her head, but did she *own it?* She picked up Pastor Tim's book now. So much of it had made sense to her on the road. It had resonated deep down inside of her. And yet to go there—*to own it*—would mean walking away from all this. She looked around her apartment. Okay, so this place wasn't that great, and her car wasn't that impressive either, but like Mossy had said, it was just the beginning. A year from now she could be living in Malibu and driving a Porsche.

But would those things make her happy?

She was pacing faster now, feeling more confused and frustrated with each step. Why was this so hard? Why was she unable to make a decision? She felt like that boat with no rudder, the one Pastor Tim talked about, being tossed and thrown back and forth with the waves. It all made her feel very, very tired and sad.

She took in a long deep breath, closing her eyes and longing for clarity. Then she fell to her knees, leaning forward on the couch with hands clasped in desperation. Quentin had been right all along. She already knew the answer. She'd

known it all along. But was she ready to own it? Was she ready
to admit that she needed God, to confess that she couldn't do
this without Him?

She bowed her head and prayed—honestly prayed. For the
first time in a long time, she poured out her heart to God, laying it all before Him, asking Him to help her, begging Him
to lead her . . . and to take her back. She didn't know how long
she prayed, but when she finished, she knew that she was not
the same person she'd been when she'd started to pray. She was
a changed person—forgiven and restored and at peace.

It was past eleven now, but she no longer felt tired. Instead,
she felt energized and hopeful. She opened her guitar case, but
before she removed her guitar, she checked the little pouch
where she kept her picks. Digging down into it, her fingers
touched the metal circle. She pulled out the ring her dad had
given her shortly after her eighteenth birthday and slipped it
on. And in that same instant it seemed to all fall into place.

She started playing the tune she'd been working on all
these months, the music she could never write the lyrics for.
But suddenly she knew the words, and it all made perfect sense.
Words and lines and music all came together, weaving themselves into the form of a complete song. She played and wrote
. . . and wrote and played . . . until it was all there. And it was
good.

# Chapter 24

Grace had no idea what to expect when she went into Larry Reynolds office. For all she knew, he might send her packing by the time she told him what was troubling her. But mostly she was relieved that he was willing to take this meeting with her. As she walked through the Sapphire lobby, she silently prayed, asking God to help her to speak honestly and to say exactly what was on her heart.

After their initial greeting and after Larry had congratulated her for climbing the charts, she spoke openly and candidly to him. She explained her concerns about singing lyrics that compromised her faith, how she was uncomfortable being photographed in a way that felt demeaning, and how she no longer wanted to perform in clubs where most of the patrons were inebriated.

"I just can't do that anymore." She choked back the emotion. "It's not who I am, not who I want to be. I can't do it anymore. I just can't." She looked directly into his eyes. "And

I feel so terrible for letting you down. Especially after you all have believed in me, you've invested in me, I don't want to let you down. I'm sorry."

"I'm sorry too, Grace."

"Really?" She studied his expression, waiting for him to start the manipulative games that Mossy sometimes played.

"I'm sorry we let you down. I don't want you to compromise yourself or your beliefs, Grace. You're a fabulous singer, and you already have a fantastic fan base. I'm pretty sure they wouldn't want you to compromise yourself either."

"Really?" she said again, almost afraid to believe his words. "So you think it's possible to succeed as a musician without compromising?"

He made a crooked grin. "Unfortunately it's not a real common scenario in this business. But, sure, it can happen. And no one's more delighted than I am when it does." He grimly shook his head. "When I hear about one of our stars—like Renae—having serious troubles, well, it just breaks my heart."

She nodded. "Yeah, me too."

"So, really, it's up to you, Grace. It's your life. You gotta call the shots."

"But what about Mossy? I feel guilty when I think about him."

"Listen, whatever you do, don't worry about old Mossy. You've resurrected his career more than you know. Seriously, Grace, you don't owe him anything."

"I don't?"

He chuckled. "If it makes you feel any better, Mossy is already scouting his next protégé—Alyssa LaRue. Or maybe she's scouting Mossy. Whatever the case, your success has really boosted Mossy's status and, unless he's a fool, he should be nothing but grateful to you. I'm just sorry he wasn't more sensitive to your needs."

"Thanks. I'm still not completely sure of what I'll do." She forced a smile as she stood. "But I do know what I *won't* do. And it's encouraging to know you understand."

"I do understand. I really do. You know what's at stake. And just know that I'm behind you whatever you decide. We'll figure it out."

He walked her to the door and, giving her a hug, told her that he was honored that she'd done her first song with Sapphire Music. "I said it when I first saw your demo, and I'll say it again—you've got real star quality, Grace."

"Thanks."

Grace knew what she had to do. It wouldn't be easy, but it was necessary. Although she didn't have an appointment, she was going to pay Mossy a visit. The receptionist greeted her as usual, complimenting Grace on her recent successes. "Is Mr. Mostin expecting you?" she asked.

"I didn't call ahead. Is he with someone?"

"No. Do you want me to let him know you're—"

"If it's okay, I can just go and announce myself."

The receptionist nodded. "Sure. Go on through, Gracie."

Grace braced herself as she walked toward his door. She could do this. God would help her. The door was ajar, and she stepped inside, preparing her speech. He was at his desk with his back to her and his feet resting on the credenza beneath his window. She was about to speak up when she heard him talking, and she assumed he was talking to her.

"I told you I'm gonna make you a star, and you better believe I'm gonna deliver on it, baby."

"But Mossy," she began.

He spun around in his chair, and she realized he was talking on the phone.

"Sorry," she said with wide eyes, mouthing, "I'll go."

"No, no, it's okay," he told her. Now he chuckled. "Hey, Alyssa, guess who's standing in my office right now. Miss Gracie Trey. Now if I could make that little girl a star, you ought to know I can do the same for you."

Grace bristled at his words but continued to smile stiffly.

"I gotta go now," he said. "But you just do like I told you, and I promise you, it's only a matter of time before you'll be nipping at Gracie Trey's heels." He laughed as he hung up. "Sorry, Gracie. I didn't mean to make you feel like Alyssa was your competition, but she was having a bad day and needed some encouragement."

"Uh, right." Grace pulled the pages of song lyrics and the flash drive from her bag, solemnly laying them on Mossy's desk.

"What's that?" He frowned.

"Listen, Mossy," she began. "I can't even begin to thank you for all you've done for me. I've given this more thought than you'll ever know, and I realized you were right."

He blinked. "Right?"

"You said the apple doesn't fall too far from the tree. And it doesn't."

"But Gracie—"

"I hope someday I can explain all my reasons for doing this, but right now, I just know I need to go home. But I want you to know that, with all my heart, I wish you the very best. Thanks for believing in me." Her eyes were filled with tears now.

"You don't know what you're doing," he said meekly.

"I do." She nodded. "Take care, Mossy." And she turned and walked out. Thankfully, he did not try to follow her.

As she walked through the lobby one last time, she knew that she had just burned a bridge, but she also knew she'd done the right thing. She knew that God was leading her . . . leading her home.

Grace clutched her guitar as she waited in the shadows backstage. She couldn't remember the last time she'd been this nervous. Even now she questioned if this was such a great idea. It was one thing to play for strangers, but playing in front of family and friends and sharing her heart like she planned on doing . . . well, that was something else completely.

She peeked out to where Pastor Tim was speaking to the congregation. From where she was standing, she could see her parents in their usual seats near the front. Of course, they had no idea what was about to happen, but she could tell that they were curious as to what Tim was saying.

"After speaking with her for some time, I was pleased to invite her here this morning. It seemed like the perfect way to end this service. So without further ado, please welcome back to our family . . . *a special guest.*"

With her guitar in hand, Grace slowly emerged from the shadows and walked out to the pulpit. With each step she silently begged God to help her do this. Her parents looked truly stunned now, and she spied Rachel literally dropping her jaw just a few rows behind them. But Pastor Tim just winked at her as she stepped up to the mic.

"Hi." She made a nervous smile, looking out over the congregation. "You probably didn't expect to see me here this morning. Most of you know I didn't exactly leave here on the best of terms. And I know along the way I hurt some of you." She looked directly at her parents, trying to control her emotions. "And for that, I just wanted to ask if you could forgive me. The problem was me. I left home to chase my dream. And I got it. Only it was the wrong dream." She had tears coming down now, and so did some of the congregation.

"So this morning, I asked Pastor Tim, and he said it was fine. He said I could play a song for you. My first song . . . that I wrote. And I want to dedicate it to my mom . . . and my dad . . . whom I love very much." She choked back a sob as she reached for her guitar. But before she strapped it on, she glanced over to the piano and then back to her dad. Setting the guitar down, she went over and sat down on the bench and started to play.

Really, the piano was the perfect instrument for this tender song. And so, putting everything she had into it, she began to sing "All I've Ever Needed" with so much heart and soul that nearly everyone in the church was crying by the time she finished. But the crying quickly subsided into joyous applause. Grace spotted her dad getting to his feet, clapping energetically, and soon the rest of the congregation was standing and clapping too. She hurried down to join her parents, happily hugging them. And then she was hugging Rachel and several other old friends. And eventually she felt someone tugging on her sleeve and looked down to see young Noah looking up at her with big eyes.

"My star guitar student," she said as she leaned down to hug him. "I'm so sorry I missed your recital." She peered into his eyes. "How did it go?"

He smiled shyly. "Okay."

She ran her hand through his hair. "Good for you. Keep practicing!"

# Chapter 25

*Two Years Later*

So much had happened in the past two years that sometimes Grace felt like she needed to pinch herself just to see if it was really real. It was as if all her dreams had actually come true . . . were coming true. But this time there were no regrets and no compromises. This time God was the one directing her path and her career.

The music pounded in her ears as Grace walked over to where Quentin was standing backstage, talking on his phone. Quentin had been managing her career for some time now, and she had no complaints. No complaints whatsoever. She glanced down at her pretty diamond engagement ring as she snuck up from behind him, planting a kiss on his cheek. He turned around and grinned. "We're up soon," he told her, then returned to whoever was on the other end.

"No, that's great news," he said into the phone. "Cool. Very cool."

Grace slipped her arm around Quentin, snuggling up close to him as she smiled over to where her band members—the same guys that helped her dad lead worship at Homewood Church—were waiting with their instruments on the sidelines. They seemed intent on watching Chris Tomlin as he wound down his performance. Chris had totally rocked the amphitheater tonight, and the audience was stoked.

"Thanks, Larry," Quentin said into the phone. "That means a lot to me."

She looked at him with curious interest. So he was talking to Larry at Sapphire Music. She wondered what was up.

But now her parents were coming over to join their little entourage.

"Hold still," her mom was saying to Dad. "Let me get this for you before you go on stage looking like a complete goofball."

"All right." He smirked at Mom as she wiped a smudge off his chin. He nodded to Grace. "We up?"

"Yeah," she told him. "Just about."

"I'm looking at a couple of new artists," Quentin was saying into the phone. "Both are strong."

Grace waved her fingers to Quentin. "Tell Larry hi," she whispered.

As Quentin delivered her greeting, Chris Tomlin exited the stage; and Quentin paused from his phone conversation to give Chris a thumbs-up. "Way to go, man."

"Thanks, Quentin." Chris nodded. "Later, man."

Quentin quickly wound up his conversation with Larry and pocketed his phone, turning to Grace with a happy grin. "Third quarter reports are in," he told her. "Larry says it looks like our division's here to stay."

She hugged him. "It's all due to your stellar leadership," she told him.

"It's your brilliant singing." Quentin kissed her.

"Hey, cut it out," Dad teased them. "You're not married yet."

Grace laughed. "Ready to rock and roll?" she asked Dad. She could hear the emcee taking over the mic now. "That Chris Tomlin never disappoints, does he?" he was saying. "As you know, this concert has been presented by Sapphire Christian Music Group," he said. "But it's not over yet. So, everybody, let's put our hands together for *The Gracie Trey Band with Johnny Trey.*"

"So let me get this straight," her dad said to Quentin with twinkling eyes. "I work for my future son-in-law?"

"Yeah, pretty much." Quentin helped Gracie strap on her guitar.

"That still sounds so weird." Grace laughed, slapping her dad on the back.

"We good?" he asked.

"You bet! Let's move it, old man!"

Pretending to walk with a limp and hunched back, Johnny headed for the stage but straightened up to his true spry self as soon as they hit the lights. As usual, the crowd came to life as the band entered the stage, clapping and yelling and cheering wildly. As the band took their places and set up, Grace looked out over the expectant faces and smiled with satisfaction— such a different atmosphere from the drinking clubs she'd been playing two years ago. She looked upward, silently thanking God that He was the one calling the shots now.

Grace and her band played with energy and enthusiasm, and the crowd zealously thanked them with noisy appreciation. But finally it was winding down, and then it was time to play the last song. Grace didn't even know where the time had gone to.

"You guys have been so great tonight," she said to the crowd. "Thanks so much for coming out and supporting us like this. And for the last song I want to leave you with something really special." Now the musicians behind her started to play the instrumental introduction to "You Never Let Go," and the crowd clapped and cheered to acknowledge they recognized it.

"This song always brings me back home," she explained. "It was written by Matt Redman. But my dad and I always played

Chris's version." She glanced at Dad, and he smiled warmly at her. "It's one of our favorites."

As Grace sang those powerful lyrics, she knew she was singing truth—every single word in this sweet song was absolutely true—*God never let go*. Despite all her mistakes and confusion and floundering, He had never let go of her. And she never wanted to let go of Him again either.